The First Book

of

The

144,000

"The Watchful One and the Tree of Life"

This book began with a Qabalistic approach to discovering the Truth and understanding the purpose of life, in allegorical form.

For over twenty-five years, I have studied Hebraic Mysticism, the Tarot, the I Ching, Norse legends, ancient stories and mythologies, Yoga, writings about psychology and philosophy from the greatest thinkers, and the Holy Scriptures.

I have interacted with Intelligences on both sides of the Veil, which has prompted me to get to know them not only collectively as "Holy Spirit" but also as unique individuals.

This book is a journey of self-discovery as I learned by parable about the demons and angels who have played an active role in my life and the Universe.'

It is the first of three foundational works: the first ten chapters.

I used the Shemhamphorash as the codex for each fallen form. This provides a starting point for discussion and writing since they are bound to the Earth.

This is the first book in a series which will tell a very true story in allegorical form. As such, the book ought to be read as if it were completely true to get the most benefit.

A reader who trusts and has faith will be edified by the Spirit. There is no claim that this book is the "most true and correct" of any book on the face of the earth, but since the foremost motive in the writing is to invoke the Holy Spirit, it might as well be the most true and correct.

Good luck!

Dedicated to my loved ones.

Table of Contents

Chapter 1 – The Crown

Foreword

Some stories begin with the archetype of the Fool or Universe, but this book starts before (and after) all that with the lucky Crown of all existence, that unknowable and ineffable seedling, and "the commencement of whirling motions" (הגלגלים ראשית).

What can we say about the great I AM, that eternal self-existent Being, who was introduced in the Old Testament (Exodus 3:4) and elsewhere. Qabalistic writers have drawn many glyphs of the Vast Countenance, and they have come up with epithets to describe this Being, this Negative Existence, who is known as The Concealed of the Concealed, The Ancient of Ancient Days, The Most Holy and Ancient One, Primordial or Smooth Point, The White Head, The Inscrutable Height, Primum Mobile....

Unknowable to man, just as the Seed is mysterious and never completely understood by a mortal mind.

It was early, very early in the morning, before the sunrise and before any creatures dared to make a sound in the obscurity of the night.

But one creature, a fallen angel with a raven's head, dared to flutter across the sky and perch atop a fence to change his view.

His name was Andras.

He was musing over the possibility of becoming great and achieving the utmost in all possibilities one day. Maybe today?

He was not alone in the world, but for the moment he had escaped the prying eyes of his many followers. There were thirty souls among them, and they all accepted Andras[1] as their leader on their missions of rampage and gluttony, in which they delighted in laying waste to their slothful and unsuspecting prey. Andras had never felt any guilt for leading these missions of murder and mayhem, for they purified the world and made it a better place, right?

But today was different, and he had some time to think.

He shuddered as he sat alone in the cold darkness.

Then he reached down and gripped his sword by the hilt and felt a wave of emptiness as images of his recent discords flashed through his mind and tormented him. He could never show this sort of infirmity or shakiness to his crew, lest they lose the faith, but he secretly began to question his own purpose and destiny.

"Am I on the right path?"

Lightning streaked across the sky and struck a tree in the prairie, sparking a small fire and sending a jolt down Andras's spine.

Then the thunder roared and rumbled loudly, shaking the ground and raising his hackles.

He shuddered and felt a twinge of fear, and remembered the adage of his uncle:

"When you are timid with fear and respect for the Almighty, you are prepared to receive the Spirit."

The thunderstorm passed, and over the next several hours Andras had some time to think about the distant future and ancient past.

And he heard a small whisper, telling him to hold onto the faith, assuring him that his wounds would be healed over time, and he would heal others in turn. The clear voice went on:

"You will understand and apply the rules of leadership, to find success in the material realm of business, through commerce, banking, and more, but to achieve this goal, you must act with subtle ingenuity and steady industry....

"Take small steps in the right direction and use the energy within your soul to achieve the utmost in possibility and greatness!

"Now is the time to cheer up, enlighten yourself for all to see, and build the great highway for your people. Check yourself, focus your thoughts, be humble and steadfast, lest the energy will pass away in a moment and lead you into years of obscurity."

The angelic messenger repeated the message three times in full.

And Andras paused to consider, and let it sink into his soul.

This was no ordinary experience, and he realized it must have been the voice of Providence.

He'd heard of such experiences before but had never actually heard the whisper audibly, so he wondered what it meant.

He felt unworthy of the task.

"I will fail in my attempt, and I cannot do it alone. I must bring around me the souls of brilliant ability."

And he didn't realize it, but in the Heavens above, at this very moment of self-doubt and awareness, the unseen angels were cheering his name, as they witnessed a transformation from Andras the Ravenhead into something much, much more.

They congratulated each other and Andras himself, filling his soul with courage and praise, and they thanked God for such great fortune to have befallen them.

For a minute, Andras felt a kinship with the angelic hosts, as if the veil separating them had been torn apart. He felt their spirit of sincere support and correction, and it taught him something about the true nature of love and devotion.

How can I remain close to this feeling of light and purpose?

He felt darkness all around, but some alien beauty and brilliance filled a single chamber with magnificent bright light around him, amidst the concourses of angelic beings.

He knew that if he wandered off away from the light, he must face terrible risks and thunderous waves of opposition.

His pride, he feared, would lead him into further oblivion, isolation, and certain peril.

He shuddered again at the thought and felt an empty surge of fear wash down his spine into his innards, and the light vanished and left him alone in the darkness.

He imagined building a fort of protection from the unforgiving elements, while exposed in this terrible blizzard of darkness and uncertainty, but he realized the effort would fail.

Then, afar off in the distance, once again he heard a voice calling after him:

"The veil is already thick, and it serves its purposes perfectly. It allows you to have free will and focus on the terrestrial realm, and work to gain your exaltation. We will communicate through the veil just enough to keep you safe and well if you will listen.

"Do not travel off into darker realms and draw up boundaries, more than is necessary. Operate within the veil with sincere devotion to achieve the utmost possibility and true greatness, making corrections and adjustments as needed."

The message stopped, then echoed in his head as before, ringing with truth and a sense of permanency. He looked around in the cold environment and saw that he was still alone, yet he knew he was not alone, and he felt grateful.

More time passed as Andras considered recent events with awe, still perched on the fence.

Then suddenly, Andras heard a beautiful and melodious sound gently resonating in the air.

What is that? He wondered as he listened for a few minutes.

The sound mutated and split into different pitches and oscillated its volume up and down, sometimes with a wavering tremolo, carrying a certain special energy that he couldn't quite identify.

And then he focused his eyes and found the source of the sound.

It was a unicorn. A single unicorn, which emerged from the wooded piney forest and entered the prairie, singing melodious tunes magically into the open air.

But it was more than just beautiful music.

The unicorn was *singing objects into existence* with his song!

They were magical, aerial, crystalline objects, rotating and playfully dancing off in every direction before dissipating and eventually vanishing, followed by a concourse of similar objects.

Andras was frozen with a mix of fear and delight, watching the mysterious unicorn miraculously wish these creations into life, and he wondered if he could touch them.

Are they real? What does it all mean?

Andras was gifted with balance and dexterity, and his mind and wits were sharp. But this new creature in front of him was so new and fantastic, and out of the ordinary, that Andras lost his grip and slipped slightly from the fence before recovering.

The creature was *directed* in a way Andras had never even imagined possible.

It flitted around, led by its head and the single spiral horn on top, always moving and somewhat restless in the moment, sometimes with jerky movements.

Andras sat nervously and motionlessly, and he hoped he would not be noticed. But the creature homed in on him and moved closer in an instant, stopping to breathe and rest its vocal cords.

With the magnificent creature before him, Andras had no idea what to say or do, but since he knew fully well that the creature was keenly aware of his presence, he mustered the courage to extend a greeting.

"Hello there!"

He tried to present himself with some confidence, hoping the creature would respect his boundaries and perhaps wander off without causing any harm. He felt a streak of fear in his bones, but he was also fascinated and wanted to learn more about this stunning unicorn. Perhaps he could learn how to perform some of its miraculous tricks.

"My name is Andras. What is your name, friend?"

The unicorn raised an eyebrow and looked closely at Andras, then shook his mane and seemed to be content with the stranger. He answered in a pleasant tone, "Hello Andras. I am Amdusias."

Amdusias[2] had been expecting to meet Andras at this time, as he had received a revelation the day before this encounter.

"Come and dine with me. We will prepare sacrament to honor my Lord and share with our followers."

Amdusias was ripe in years, and he had a glow of contented wisdom about him; the sort of glow that comes with experience and success in life. He exuded a gentle temperament with his unassuming sincerity and respect.

As they sat down to feast, Amdusias began with a prayer to invoke the Holy Spirit to reside with them, direct their minds, accept their humble offerings, and bless the food.

Then he counseled all who were gathered to use their intellect to make good choices and do good in the world around them.

Finally, he asked God, *"What are your enlightened requirements at this time?"*

His sincerity was powerful and true, such as no man could doubt his intentions. It was clear that this conversation with his Lord was easy and familiar, like a personal conversation with an old true friend, with no pomp nor vanity, but rather a relaxed and familiar yet bold tone. Each of them felt the Spirit descend upon them to lift their minds and hearts, as he spoke.

And during the meal, Amdusias told stories about some of the brave adventuring spirits of the past, who had built wooden crafts to float upon the dangerous waters. These vessels were floating temples designed to withstand against the raging seas, and to carry their passengers safely to a promised land after an extended voyage. "The legendary architects who constructed these ships were selfless and directed by a holier sphere of beings who watch over the minds and welfare of mankind."

He explained that the next chapter in history would require similar dedication and effort to fulfill the purposes of the Lord on the Earth, for His people. There would be some difficult trials ahead, causing anxiety and fear as we change and move toward greater stability. Each one of us will need to exercise great firmness and correctness, and rewards will be great for those who endure!

He also declared that Andras would be made king of the land, which came as quite a shock to the young Ravenhead.

Amdusias did not wish to install a king over the land, but his people had petitioned him for a king. He warned the people about the potential pitfalls and the great price of having a king, such as great taxes, drafts, wars, and industry, and all other forms of subjection. But they preferred this to the alternative and wished to sustain a king over the land.

He was still reluctant to anoint a king, but his Lord instructed him to follow the will of the people, for they were lost, and it was the lesser of multiple evils. The people were alienated and confused about what they ought to do and were doomed to disintegrate entirely without the installation of a king and his large entourage. It was not the ideal scenario, but the unification of the nation-state would depend upon it in the short term.

The pride and vanity of men would lead to bickering and strife within the nation, he explained. Renegade warriors would head off into ill-conceived battles without cause, reflecting poorly on the rest of the nation.

"But good men will stand out with brilliance and courage, bringing healing in their wings as they care for their brothers," he continued. "They will glow with the healthy perspiration of good labors, inspiring many others with their work and fruit.

"Some idle bystanders will watch and scoff from the distance," he continued slowly, "but eventually, with faith or compulsion, they will all learn to follow their king and his chosen ones."

[1] In the *Shemhamphorash* of the *Goetia*, *Andras* appears as the sixty-third among the seventy-two spirits. He is small and meek, yet powerful and proud in his own right, dangerous to a careless man who isn't aware of his discords, which are like the mayhem of Loki in the Norse legends. He and his 30 legions would easily lay waste to careless or slothful observers.

The only hope for Andras and for Man is to seek the infinitely good nature within himself, to be timid with fear while he works out his exaltation with trembling, which prepares him to receive healing and instruction from the angels. Andras is very active and industrious, yet subtle and ingenious, showing extraordinary energy with the utmost possibility and greatness in the moment. He leads and enlightens us all as we build the great highway. But his energy will pass away in a moment and lead to years of obscurity if he does not watch his pride and focus!

His angelic identity before the Fall was known as *Anyael*.

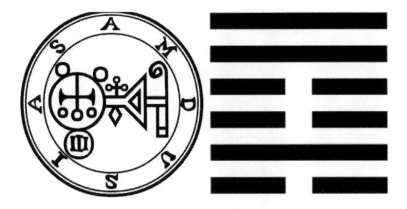

[2] *Amdusias* seems to have unlimited yet specialized and advanced powers of perception, not only in the audio range but also – by extension – in the visual. To a blind man, Amdusias may seem to be somewhat of a simpleton at first, because he makes strange noises which sound like ramblings of a mad beast. But he has the power to produce physical forces and objects through the force of sound. He was known as *Aychael* before the Fall and became a mighty Duke, sophisticated and complex in design and purpose. He is wise and a counterpart of the Crown in the eternal scheme of things, and he will answer to man when called upon. The most astute listener can hear his songs, but most often the clearest answers arrive in the visual range, through visions or illumination or flashes of light to draw our attention to whatever is most important at the current time.[3]

[3] But when communicating with any of these spirits, an aspirant should first be very careful to invoke the Holy Spirit to oversee and direct this communication. He should use his own mind and intellect to make good choices and do well in the world, asking questions such as the Duke asked during his prayer:

"What are the enlightened requirements of the Spirit of God? What is this so-called Kingdom of God? And what is my role in that Kingdom today?"

Chapter 2 – Wisdom

Foreword

In the Norse tradition, Frigga or Frigg is the second and principal wife of Odin, the queen of the gods, who spins golden thread and weaves clouds for the world. She does not speak often, but when she does her words are full of wisdom, patience, and strength – the strength that comes with abstract intelligence. She comes under many names such as Holda, Astara, or Bertha, associated with the Birch tree and the primitive trigram known as "sun" in the I Ching, which is the wood and the wind in one.

She prefers the solitude and retreat of the marshes, though she remains vibrant and fastidious in her artwork. Her dress is variable like the sky, and she specializes in "immovable" lights, which are represented in modern Freemasonry by the square, level, and plumb line. We use these tools to make precise plans and take exact measurements in the geometric plane of existence. And yet, she is also the mistress of pratyahara (abstraction), through which her senses turn inward, like a turtle withdrawing its head and limbs back into its shell for introspection.

Here in this chapter, we meet the living incarnation of Frigga, which entered the third dimension as the fallen spirit known as Marbas, and which found redemption and its True Higher Self known as Mahashiah.

So, amid the prevailing dispersion in the land, Amdusias took the necessary steps to this coronation for the security of the nation, and he received the blessings of the Lord. Despite his earlier reservations, he felt no regrets and was willing to put his whole heart into Andras and the future of his leadership.

But time passed, and the fledgling kingdom of Andras would not last long, nor even gain a foothold, because he was not careful about the attention to details when obeying and sustaining the Word of God, as communicated to him by the holy orator and prophet Amdusias.

Amdusias was also a fallible creature, who was prone to make mistakes and erred in the other direction, by taking the Word received in his revelations too literally at times. So Andras and Amdusias clashed.

Andras refused to obey the command of Amdusias to demolish an enemy camp, down to the last breathing being, and instead he showed mercy on a few and saved animals sacrificial offerings.

So, Amdusias was furious and finished the task himself. He felt justified in carrying out the Lord's command to slaughter every one of the enemies, because they had previously been ruthless in massacring the sons and daughters of many of his own people.

Therefore, Amdusias cut off all ties with Andras, removed him as king, and went out in search of a new king. And they each lived with pride and enmity between them, constantly worried about what the other may do in retaliation.

But Amdusias, despite his failings, was still favored of the Lord because he prayed often and put himself in the proper position to receive revelations and visions, and he strove to serve the Lord. He taught and practiced that obedience was far more important than any idolatrous sacrificial offering, and he looked for a wise king to secede Andras.

He asked to know by which name he should call the Lord, and the Lord answered, saying, *"My name is manifold, and no man may speak it, but you may call me Marbas-Mahashiah[1], as I am your true Savior, and I enlighten the one who looks upon Me."*

Sometimes Amdusias's mind was too weak to function properly and receive the inspired instruction, so his Lord would leave physical cues to help direct his pathways. Marbas-Mahashiah knew the future, and he led a vast number of attendant servants and handmaidens who performed their miracles among mankind, occasionally leaving golden or copper thread to lead the way.

Marbas-Mahashiah also loved the wind and wooden creations, and sometimes he left flaxen eggs or birch seedlings in the path of Amdusias, and other subtle reminders of Nature's resurrection, as he weaved atmospheric clouds for the world.

Amdusias sought diligently and learned more about his Lord, Marbas-Mahashiah. He received guidance from the immovable lights of the heavens, and crafted tools to assist in measuring and carrying out his precise planning in the worldly plane.

The messages from Marbas-Mahashiah were often abstract and caused Amdusias to turn inwardly for a greater understanding, his mind to follow and imitate these internal senses. Having a supreme mastery of the third dimension and its mechanical arts, he advised Amdusias on diverse subjects such as the cause and cure for diseases, High Science, sacred philosophy and theology, liberal arts, shapeshifting, and the power of the Word – through speech and writing.

He advised Amdusias that speech was more than just a wild act of creation, but rather a most powerful tool to discern the truth, leading to powerful action. "Actions speak louder than words," he proclaimed, "but any word or action, however small and seemingly insignificant, is powerful and a part of the Whole."

He counseled Amdusias to work and think, to stand up for what is right and good, and to find and uphold the balance between faith, reason, liberty, and equality.

"I charge you to use the power of the Word wisely, mediated and guided by a sense of brotherly love."

Marbas-Mahashiah could take any shape he wished, but most often chose to represent himself in the form of a great lion king, with thirty-six hosts following behind. And he taught Amdusias to transform his unicorn appearance as well, to that of a man.

"Fear nothing but the LORD, hunger nothing, and help many!"

Marbas-Mahashiah listened well to Amdusias because Amdusias was a sincere seeker. He responded by teaching Amdusias to learn and enjoy the simple pleasures along with the great and noble truths of life. They discussed this at length while amidst the birch tree grove, the great hall in the marshes.

Meanwhile, one day while Andras wandered about in exile with his flock of followers, seeking for a fresh carcass to devour, he heard a wild noise in the distance, braying and cackling.

And upon further investigation, he saw a queer peacock making the noise, frolicking about in the brush, seeming to enjoy himself as he flipped around and let out all these wild sounds.

But the peacock noticed the approach of Andras, and he stopped and stared, confused and frightened by the menacing look on his dark raven face.

"Tell me, peacock, where may I find a place to take rest?"

The peacock immediately took on a ruddy young human with wide lustrous iridescent eyes and an inquisitive look on his face.

"Do you mean to find a particular place in the heavens?" the peacock-boy asked awkwardly.

"No, young man, I am seeking refuge for myself and my armies on this Earth, so that we can rebuild the kingdom that is still rightfully mine to rule. I am Andras. And what is your name?"

The boy was a bit unsure how to relate with this Ravenhead, but he cocked his head and answered. "My name is Andrealphus. We are the master of geometry and heavenly mensuration."

Andras paused to consider the similarity of their names. "Mensuration?"

"Yes, we use mathematics to determine the nature and map of the stars, the planets, and other objects in our material universe. We understand the times and seasons perfectly, and we apply this knowledge to any living creature who walks upon the earth, to determine the future number of his days... and more."

"Hmm." Andras paused again. "So, tell me, what is the future number of *my* days? How long will I live?"

"Ah." Andrealphus[2] smiled, then continued, "For that, we must get to know each other a little more...."

So, they began to walk and talk.

And by the end of the day, they were exhausted from all the conversation, analysis, equations, and many variables discussed. It turned out that Andrealphus could not give Andras a specific date and time, but only a range depending on several key pivotal decision points in Andras's future.

"So, you mean to say that the future is not yet set? My free will and choices can make a difference?"

"Within a specific range, yes. The big picture is predetermined, but your choices will make a difference within that context."

Andras was fascinated to learn that despite this free will, Andrealphus could predict with astonishing specifics about the nature and time of his passing, and he threw himself into calculations with a passion. This was not just a mechanical operation for Andrealphus, but an overwhelming emotional rollercoaster. He even held back a few tears as he flashed back to his former glory, before his fall to the mortal terrestrial realm, and he pleaded with Andras to accept the allocated number of his days with gladness and joy.

"Be grateful, Andras, for the mercy of the Creator, and apply your heart unto wisdom in the service of other souls in need! Uplift and strengthen the United Order of living beings, as we are all spirit children of the eternal and living God."

The child spoke with the authority of an angel, mild and youthful yet ageless in wisdom. He went on:

"Trust in His infinite wisdom and integrity, by which He fulfills every promise perfectly and completely. Emulate His example.

Fulfill your bargains and obey the commandments, for the Supreme Being directs and enlightens your mind and your eyes, and He helps you find success on your seafaring adventures."

Andras stopped him. "Seafaring?"

Andrealphus seemed not to hear the question, and he began to tremble as he lapsed into a darker state of mind. He fell to the earth and repeatedly beat his fist against the dirt, until his hand began to throb, and his body was exhausted. He wiped a tear from his eye, then passed out in exhaustion with a thud on the soft ground.

"What happened?" asked Andras, in a low whisper to himself.

Andrealphus had been so eager to serve and comply with the requests and questions of Andras that he had turned the crank a bit too far, and he lost his grip on reality as he struggled with complex mathematical models in his mind. These calculations were too much for him to handle.

Like the wind, or like a tree branching off into every possible nook and cranny all in one moment, considering every possible outcome all at once, his normal nature of harmony and deference became stretched a bit too thinly. He had tried to comprehend too much, too fast, and he collapsed in exhaustion.

Andras felt somehow responsible and tended to his care for a while, until he woke up once again.

"Andrealphus? What happened? Are you okay?"

Andrealphus had recoiled into his peacock form again and was deadlocked with fear. "Oh!" he clamored, "Went just a bit too far that time! Won't do that again!"

"Do what?"

"Penetrated a bit too far that time, see? Everything is fine now."

Aldrealphus was eager to please Andras and felt embarrassed by the whole episode and his fainting spell. His mind occasionally flipped into a violent sort of overload or collapse, and now he stood petrified with fear, wanting to share his great enthusiasm, but fearing Andras's reaction.

The awkward moment didn't last long before some bristling in the nearby shrubs warned of an intruder, and a strange dog-like creature appeared on the scene with a low growl.

This creature was no ordinary canine. He was massive in size and had a pair of white wings on his back, like a gryphon, and as he stood up on his hind legs, he flared his wings to demonstrate his power, and he growled lowly again with a peculiar vibration that rattled the bones of both Andras and Andrealphus.

Fresh blood dripped from his teeth, and he pranced left and right to show off his dexterity and readiness.

Andrealphus was locked with fear, but Andras stood up straight and took a firm stance, seemingly unintimidated by the creature. He took a large breath in through his raven beak.

"Fear not," proclaimed Andras boldly, "for I know this beast and his kind."

From out of the woods emerged a pack of similar creatures, smaller yet still ferocious, thirty-six in number.

"*Glasya-Labolas,*" proclaimed Andras, "have you forgotten who you are? You are among the fallen of Nith-Hayach, and I hereby command you to stand down."

And with a whimper, the creature immediately stopped to reflect, sat down on his hind haunches, and licked his chops, realizing that Andras had the advantage. He motioned with his eyes to the hounds behind him, and they all relaxed their stances in turn.

Glasya-Labolas[3], as he was called, was awakened from a trance, and his eyes brightened with a blue hue. "Thank you Andras. It's been a long while. And who is your companion?"

Andrealphus gasped a sigh of relief and returned to human form, having collected his wits once again.

"We are Andrealphus of Damabyah."

"Ah yes," muttered the hound, "then we serve the same Lord. I welcome you, and I apologize for my poor approach. It seems the bloodlust had hold of my soul. I thank you, Andras, for releasing me from its grasp."

The three and their hosts made camp and discussed their plans, while eating a great meal. The hounds brought in their kill by the cartload, which provided an excellent feast for all, as they gave thanks and dedicated their energy to fulfilling Divine Will.

Andrealphus felt somewhat better now, but he was still paranoid about the hounds and their vile nature. He respected their size and dexterity, and even their wisdom, but he considered their wisdom to be lesser or darker than his own. And the more he dwelled on these many concerns, he felt uneasy within himself, at war with his own dark side, and unable to think clearly.

But Glasyas-Labolas, the gryphon-hound, began to open himself up more to the group about his hopes and ambitions, and he was lavish with his praise of the Grand Creator. He even broke down into sad tears as he expressed regret about his animal instincts.

"I know so much about science and the arts, the past and future," he lamented, "but ultimately it avails nothing and has no good use without a strong leader to guide my thoughts. It seems we, the hounds of the Nith-Hayach, are merely followers."

"Merely?" Andras interrupted. "You sell yourself short, friend. You are the best sort of companion, and we all need guidance!

"You lost control, and like many of us you needed a firm voice to shake your soul and remind you of your true calling in life."

He paused, then continued, "But you came to your senses and now you uplift others with insight and vivid revelations. We all see the sincere emotion and your strong desire to suffer for the greater good with a glad heart, with uprightness and rectitude!"

The gryphon-hound was reticent but accepted the compliment, and thanked Andras for the kind words. At first, he sat brooding with heavy introspection, wanting to control things that were out of his control, but he resolved internally to let go and just relax. He was wound up tightly from the hunt, and he needed to slow down and let himself and others catch up.

Andrealphus finally began to relax as well, and he added, "Glasya-Labolas, we see potential for extraordinary greatness in you in your future. You will follow conditions and requirements of light and high glory, be it celestial or terrestrial, and the Spirit will enliven and quicken your soul if you are firm and correct in upholding the divine law."

He paused, then continued, "But you must decide now which law you will follow, for you can only follow one. You will face the crossroads many times in your life, and at each crossroads you must decide whether you will follow the law of youthful folly or the law of mature wisdom. You will find your greatest potential as you use strength to support the weak with perfect sincerity, just as an older brother would provide motive force for his younger sister."

It was an excellent meeting between these three leaders of legions, promising good fortune in the future. They dwelled together and built a community over the next several years.

Marbas-Mahashiah looked over them, ensuring their success by providing plenty of flax and sheep in the surrounding lands. They used the wool fibers to spin string and created many fabrics and other fine linens, and all sorts of materials to use.

One major project in the land was that of building a tabernacle to resemble the original temple, which required a colossal effort to construct and decorate with proper coverings, drapes, and so on. Andras had parted ways with Amdusias the prophet, but he still believed it was important to dedicate his kingdom to the Lord. So, he went to great lengths to understand and reproduce the ordinances of the original priesthood in this land.

So, a new group of servants was set apart to tend to the temple and its sacred sacrificial offerings, to carry emblems of the Lord and His covenants, and so on. These servants worked in shifts to ensure that the fires of the temple would always remain lit, the lavers full and clean, and the sacrifices separated and offered in holiness, as well as possible. Some were set apart as scribes who recorded the daily activities and history of the people, and others administered blessings among the various tribes in their camps.

Overall, the small kingdom began to thrive like clockwork, a well-oiled machine with gears and wheels within wheels, each person tending to his responsibilities with a positive attitude. They made light work of the heaviest tasks because as they worked together, specializing yet also helping each other.

Some were merchants and others were architects, inventing and conducting their affairs great and small. Others were engineers, artisans, musicians, scientists, teachers, students, mechanics, messengers, and so on.

The society was based upon principles of charity and welfare, with special care provided for the widows, orphans, and others who needed help. They established excellent customs to honor their lost warriors and others who passed away and went the way of the earth. Laws and customs were enacted to protect the innocent and the weak, and great order prevailed in the land. There were some outcasts and disabled people, unable to work, so they created special camps and provided food to help and rehabilitate these unfortunate souls.

The angels administered to the people often, and the people rejoiced in these visitations and miracles of healing.

Marbas-Mahashiah continued to learn and grow in the process, and he felt much joy as his people matured, for he considered them to be his people. He became more responsible and aware of his actions, and he exerted his influence while respecting the free will of each individual therein. He allowed them to choose and make mistakes on their own, from which to learn and grow.

He learned that he is powerful and has great influence over all, yet the wheel as a whole is only as effective as its inner parts – the wheels within the wheels of his society. So, he sought to serve and love his people, and they loved him in return, in a symbiotic relationship which made him very proud. And yet, Marbas-Mahashiah also felt humbled and inadequate compared to the Supreme Being, Whom he sought to emulate.

He organized his plan in accordance with the Masloth, which is known as the Zodiac in modern times. He observed the seasons and cycles and the heavenly influences, from the macroscopic scale down to the microscopic. The people loved his leadership because of his keen awareness of the delicate balance of this universal wheel of life, leading to good things such as health, sanitation, and uprightness.

He set the standard and showed his people how to make changes – with absolute sincerity and honor in words. He showed them what it meant to be a father, active in the lives of his children, and one in purpose with his companions. He was (and still is) abstract in his thinking, as he deals with ordering the infinities and the supremely high calling to lead his people.

Marbas-Mahashiah loved (and still loves) all mankind, but he especially enjoys and favors the arts of spinning, housekeeping, and sympathizing with those who mourn. He considers these to be among the most noble human activities. And he watches the internals of his mind play out in the external world.

The people named their civilization Mahashiah after their Lord, and they spread out with many cities and states across the land, connected by roads, viaducts, highways, byways, and so on. And they established a strong army to protect their borders.

[1] *Marbas* is the great president and fifth in the Shemhamphorash. He has a supreme mastery of the third physical dimension and its mechanical arts, including the causes and cures of diseases and shape shifting. He often chooses the form of a great lion to lead his thirty-six legions and perform his work, and he is specially endowed with the ability to take any shape in his mind.

We should call upon Marbas to take the form of his highest self, *Mahashiah*, the Savior who enlightens the one who calls and looks upon him. Mahashiah is ascribed to and described in the thirty-fourth Psalm of David as the one who shows the way to eternal life with the Lord, fearing nothing save the Lord himself, hungering nothing, and helping many.

He governs High Science, Occult philosophy, theology, and the liberal arts. He listens to a sincere seeker and teaches us to learn and enjoy the simple pleasures along with noble truths.

[2] *Andrealphus* is listed as the sixty-fifth fallen spirit, who commands thirty legions of infernal spirits. Like Marbas and many of the spirits to be discussed here, he is a shapeshifter, but he is limited to specific forms such as the peacock and human, which are his favorite sorts of beings. He is also quite fond of making wild and loud noises, yet when he settles down and a sincere student asks for instruction, he can teach all the subtleties of geometry and astronomy (e.g., mensuration) with eloquence and near-perfect accuracy.

In the ninetieth Psalm of David is a prayer of Moses which speaks powerfully and attunes our minds to the highest glorified form of Andrealphus, known as *Damabyah*. His knowledge about geometry in the stars may be applied to us as individuals, whose days are limited and numbered unto the eternal Lord.

"How long?" we might ask.

The best we can do is pray that the Lord will teach us to accept the number of our days with gladness, expressing gratitude for his mercy, applying our hearts unto wisdom and service of others in need, and strengthening each other as One United Order.

As we trust in the infinite wisdom and integrity of Damabyah, he will always fulfill his part of every holy bargain, directing and enlightening our minds and eyes, helping us find success on our adventures on the waters.

The shapeshifting Andrealphus is characterized by deference, pliable and flexible like the wind, which finds its way into every nook and cranny. What happens above happens below, and due to this effective alignment, there is progress and achievement due to iterative corrections.

At first it may seem that there is nothing grand nor amazing here, but an interesting story unfolds as we learn from our mistakes, resorting to various means such as divination, violence, sacrifice, entertaining guests (especially after a hunt), planning ahead and communicating change, then reanalyzing again, etc. The major risk of Andrealphus, which led to his fall, is that of overexertion and exhaustion. He looked beyond the mark and ran faster than he had strength until he collapsed and was no longer able to penetrate effectively, having spread himself too thinly.

[3] *Glasya-Labolas* is the twenty-fifth fallen spirit who commands thirty-six legions, and the author of bloodshed and manslaughter. His appearance is that of a might dog with a gryphon's wings, highly energetic, capable of amazing feats of strength, dexterity, and dark wisdom. Those who commune with him may become temporarily invisible due to his cloaking effect, but they will feel paranoid and at war with the world and oneself, despite intense temporary love that may flare up between his hosts.

He knows a lot about science and the arts, the past and future, but the knowledge is relatively useless and avails very little until we ask him to take and remember his true and original self, and high identity, Nith-Hayach, who loves the Lord with all his heart and openly declares His miracles with praise and celebration.

And he is great a friend to others, offering service and uplifting them with insightful and vivid revelations.

Glasya-Labolas is not often bubbling with joy and excitement, and sometimes he breaks down into tears, overcome with emotion and desire to suffer with the Lord in a glad heart.

And yet, even in his emotion, there is uprightness and rectitude. He feels the universe around him with sensitivity in his limbs, his hands, and his head, and he holds the key to introspective self-knowledge in his breast. He comprehends weaknesses in others and knows when to release control and be patient for others to catch up.

So, those who follow the conditions and requirements of the light and glory afforded them will receive great progress and success in the celestial and earthly realms. There will be no error if one is firm and correct in upholding the divine law, allowing the Spirit of Covenant to enliven and quicken the soul – the spirit and the body working together as one unified entity. One must decide which law to follow; that of youthful folly or mature wisdom.

Glasya-Labolas reaches his highest potential as he places his strength beneath the weak ones, providing motive force as an older brother would for his youngest sister, with sincerity.

Chapter 3 – Understanding

Foreword

Having learned that there are balancing forces within the soul, and recognizing the necessity to subdue one's carnal passions, we return to the mind to control the energy through breathwork.

Study of pranayama generally assumes one has already acquired the firm posture, and I will proceed with an assumption that the reader is aware of his posture and prepared to make this next step toward the control of inhalation and exhalation movements.

The legend of Thor is fascinating, and it establishes him as a principal god among the hosts of the Aesir, shouldering his lightning hammer in his mighty chariot, drawn by his goats, crackling and gnashing with sparks. Unlike his cousin Frey, Thor is impetuous and unpredictable, moody yet determined when he makes up his mind. He journeyed to Jotunheim and took on the giants, proving himself as fearless and powerful leader, yet he was unable to overthrow the kingdom entirely due to their evil tricks. So, he compromised and made peace with the giants.

Thor's sacred tree is the oak, which worshippers would burn ceremoniously on his principal festival, the yuletide, to bring some light and warmth to the season.

"The force of electricity [is] analogous to... sympathy, [by] which great thoughts or base suggestions, utterances of noble or ignoble natures, flash instantaneously over nerves of nations," per Albert Pike. This is the force of Thor which can inspire and facilitate great changes in individuals and great nations.

The gift of Thor is no less than the ability to generate light, which places him at the center of worship and connection to other deities of light including Horus, Hermes, Heracles, etc., which are inseparably linked to regeneration and resurrection,, inspiration toward intelligence, and so on. It's easy to see why the ancient Nordics worshipped Thor until King Olaf the Second removed his shrines and revealed the superstitious traditions of Thor worship. He is the eldest brother, and he is associated with the primitive trigrammatic elemental "kăn", which is symbolized by the thunderous movement of the great azure yellow dragon, who rules the heavens.

Thor took a dim view of Loki's lies and the dark intelligence of the dwarves, yet he was forward-thinking enough to forgive them wherever possible and establish mutually beneficial agreements. His ability to forgive Loki led to some significant and admirable tools and weapons and crafts, developed by the clever dwarves, such as Thor's powerful hammer Mjolnir, Odin's ring and spear (Draupnir and Gungnir), Frey's ship and golden-bristled boar (Skidbladnir and Gullinbursti).

Now we will meet Samigina, the "horse with a hoarse voice," who is strong like Thor, yet – also like Thor -- he seems to have trouble accepting his birthright. But like the ancient King David in the famous Sixth Psalm, Samigina desires to praise the Lord, and he trusts in the Lord's saving and protecting grace, through which he realizes his Higher Self, which is known as Aylimiah.

Aylimiah is also known as Allah.

Meanwhile, the mighty speaker and prophet

Amdusias occasionally travelled through the land of Mahashiah, disguised as a common man to mingle, because he delighted in the children of men.

And one day, while meditating in a grove of trees, he assumed his original unicorn form and prayed for guidance.

And, while caught up in fervent prayer, suddenly out of thin air, a brilliant white horse-like creature came galloping down from the clouds with the rumble of thunder to follow.

But before Amdusias could react to this mysterious creature, it crashed loudly on the ground, then stood up and transformed itself into the form of a massive man, wielding a large hammer, and raised the hammer up to the sky.

The hammer glowed with electric intensity and emitted dancing sparks all around, rumbling like thunder and streaking the air with light as it moved.

Amdusias was awestruck and dared not to move, but he heard some rustling, so he looked around quickly and watched keenly as the shrubs and stalks began to sprout and branch out quickly, thorns and vines jetting out every which way at a quickened rate, as if they were stimulated or threatened by the force.

But then the thunder stopped, and the rustling stopped, and all went silent as the giant horseman relaxed his position and spoke with the authority of thunder in his voice:

"The Lord has sent me to advise you, Amdusias, because you are particularly fit and called to serve as a mentor for my child, whose name shall be Orias."

Amdusias was transfixed with awe as he continued.

"My name is Samigina, and I am sent to teach you about the liberal sciences. I come to you in peace."

Samigina[1] proceeded to show Amdusias many things, and he seemed to enjoy the sharing and teaching.

But eventually he became flustered.

He muttered a curse and groaned with displeasure, as if he were tormented by some unseen force around him.

This seemed strange to Amdusias, since he reasoned that this powerful being Samigina would have progressed beyond mere moodiness or vulnerability. But sure enough, Samigina had lost his temper and stooped to his knees to try to collect his emotions, then began to breathe deeply and rhythmically. The process was exhausting and left Samigina in tears.

He regained his composure, he apologized to Amdusias for the interruption, and tried to explain himself.

"Sometimes I forget who I really am, Amdusias, as I recount the stories of the dead and the fate of man, which weigh heavily on my soul. But who am I to question the eternal scheme of our Grand Architect, for he is the Lord of the Living. I know much about the stories of the dead, and it weighs down on me. Let us praise the Lord and trust in his saving and protecting grace."

His prayer that followed was profound and sincere. The heavens and earth shook, and the air moved, as he spoke with eloquence.

Amdusias was amazed and humbled that this powerful creature would humble himself and show such reverence and deference toward his Creator. And Amdusias started to breathe steadily, no longer intimidated, but rather inspired with the motive force. He learned that Samigina was a fallen spirit of Ahlimiah, sent to Earth to fulfill an obligation. He is a great builder and architect, who works mightily and inspires others to follow; a begotten son of the Supreme Being of the Universe. He could take on various forms including the horse, human, and a mighty flying dragon, and he shone brightly with azure and yellow hues, occasionally flaring red as his voice shook with a cautionary tone.

He warned Amdusias about traitors and treachery in his midst, then advised him that Andras would need help in his voyages.

Then he explained that he had work to do in another land, a land of giants, and suddenly, in a flash, his heavenly chariot appeared before them, drawn by a pair of goats, crackling with sparks.

"There will be peace in the land, but there are battles to fight before we may declare victory overall," he said with a sideways glance toward the nearby grove of trees.

"I leave you this sacred oak tree in the grove," he said, as the gigantic oak sprouted with bristling branches and caused the soil around the trunk to break up and churn with incredible force.

Amdusias felt an empathic and electric connection with the tree, and he perceived the great thoughts and noble nature of the tree stirring in his mind. And he began to feel ashamed of the base suggestions and less-noble nature within his own selfish mind, which flashed instantaneously over the nerves of the nations through an invisible network. He felt connected and accountable to the higher intelligence, the mind of the world, and witnessed the miracles of creation and resurrection appear before his eyes.

He was grateful for such a divine revelation, and he inspired to fulfill his calling with utmost dedication. He was eager to learn more about Orias, mentioned by Samigina, and live up to the lofty expectations placed upon him.

Samigina readied his goats for departure, then stopped to share a final word. "It is your responsibility and privilege to exercise balance between justice, reason, and mercy. You should use your freedom and independence of thought to ask questions and take personal accountability for thoughts and actions. Even the Master spends much time at the trestle board using geometry, mathematics, and pure reasoning to draft His plans.

"You must practice discipline and seek diligently to understand the mind of the Grand Master, who animates all life. *But first and foremost, let your reasoning be shocked and even paralyzed in the face of the wondrous creation and the eternal round of time and space, giving precedence to pure faith.*"

Then Samigina closed his eyes and took a deep breath through his nose, opened his glowing-white eyes, and departed. He held up the hammer up once again, and lightning struck the ground from its tip, causing another loud rumble of thunder as a new creature appeared where the lightning had struck.

"Behold, I give you Orias."

Orias[2] entered the scene boldly and confidently, swaying his lioness head from side to side to observe his new surroundings. His body was built like that of a horse, and his long tail like that of a massive serpent, and in his right hand he held two hissing writhing serpents, apparently agitated, nipping at each other.

And behind him were thirty additional creatures, much smaller but similar in form to Orias himself, standing by at full alert, staring around wildly at their new surroundings.

"So, this is the place appointed by our father," Orias uttered in a deep voice, with noticeable tension in the air, breathing uneasily.

Amdusias stood startled for a few seconds, and then realized he needed to say something. So, he cleared his throat and declared with confidence, "Hello Orias. Your arrival was announced by your father, and my calling is to serve as your mentor while you abide with us here. How may I assist?"

Orias trembled nervously as he observed his new environment. Then he breathed deeply and shook his tail all about wildly, before regaining his composure somewhat. The two snakes in his right hand looked around and hissed their disapproval of the uncomfortable circumstances, as if to ward off any potential threats in the area.

Clearly something was wrong here, and Amdusias sought to settle everybody down a bit. So, he bowed his head, lowering his horn as a sign of deference and peace. "We mean no harm, Orias. Please...."

Orias took a breath to calm himself, and a stern yet impassioned look crossed his broad lioness face. His brow was still furrowed in dismay, and his eyes brightened with longing and desperation. "You are Amdusias of Aychael?"

"Yes, I am," Amdusias said with his head still bowed, having transformed into human form now.

Orias transformed as well, taking on the appearance of a man, yet he retained with many of his previous unique characteristics.

"I am Orias of Herehael, sent by Samigina of the Ahlimiah to lead a great work in these lands. I apologize for my foreboding form and introduction, but I've learned to distrust new territories and strange people.... But I understand that you are engaged in an important work here, and we are here to assist you."

Amdusias felt unprepared for the offer but knew this was no time to hesitate, so he spoke up once again:

"It is wonderful that you would you join in our efforts, Orias. We must prepare for adventures and form an alliance with the previous king Andras. We will need to build a port town for shipbuilding and everything else to support this bold venture. Will you support the work?"

"Yes, I will," responded Orias. "Praise the Lord, whose miracles grace us all the day long!"

One of his thirty followers seemed upset with the turn of events and dared to challenge his master: "Master Orias, we just arrived hungry and tired, and you commit us to this new work...?"

"Humble yourself and prepare for the work," responded Orias. *"Let us cultivate our virtues and examine our faults, and move swiftly with the changes, for the movements are temporary and will not last forever. We must act, or we will miss the chance...."*

And then he sprang into action, taking notes and measurements as he quickly moved about the land, practicing what he preached. His demeanor completely changed, and his mannerisms became more methodical and balanced now as he moved. His snakes clung tightly to him and raveled themselves around his body, watching inquisitively and holding still as Orias worked with both hands to take his measurements.

"The heavenly bodies are in a special agreement, and we will be blessed with favors from both friends and foes in the near future. Treasure is in store...," Orias trailed off.

"What sort of treasure?" asked Amdusias.

"Well, the treasure bestowed by the stars, the planets, and all their virtues, which will lead to great success in various ways, but I find most interest in channeling these many virtues into books and banks, since these will translate into every other form of success in our burgeoning society."

He continued to take measurements upward toward the sky, confirming and nodding his head as he peered through the lens of an odd-looking instrument, something like a sextant yet far more complex.

Amdusias was startled by his swift yet calculated movements, and he tried to keep up as Orias measured and took notes in a neat and orderly fashion. He took all his notes upon a glowing tablet with his fingers. And after drawing his first set of plans, he reviewed them quickly and handed them to his first assistant, who received the plans, made a facsimile on his own device, and began discussing them with his peers, considering how to begin implementation.

Orias retrieved his tablet and started working on another plan, this time a ledger with financial plans and transactional records.

Amdusias had never witnessed such miraculous technology, and he marveled at its mysterious function, which seemed to cooperate with the mind of Orias, behaving predictively and interactively as a lifeform would act, with a mind of its own. It could even change shapes, stretch, and roll up into a scroll, which was useful for portability.

The first plan was for a viaduct, along with roads and waterways connecting to a neighboring city. It also contained the precise location for a water well, destined to become the center of a city. Orias's team made no delays and began to inspire others around as they moved efficiently.

*"I've learned, dear Amdusias, I must keep my ego in check,
for it loves to lie and create a risk for my soul,
as demons to assume possession."*

Amdusias stared, interested but bewildered by this odd comment.

*"... And these demons will only make me ugly, deformed and
grotesque like their own tortured souls...,"* continued Orias with
a serious laugh, as if thinking back on a sour memory.

He paid no attention to the bustling and movement going on all
around him.

"The ego cares about temporal things, and it feels pain when it
loses those things. I've lost many things, dear Amdusias, but in
the end it matters not, for we will always have the things we
need in the moment, to carry out the plans of the Almighty."

The most amazing thing began to happen around Orias and his
legion of men. Every form of plant life in the vicinity began to
sprout up and grow at an accelerated rate, in the same way the
oak tree had sprouted up in the grove, but to a lesser degree.

Amdusias could hardly believe his eyes. Life was in full bloom,
fertile and strong, and he could feel the strange energy stirring
within his own body as well.

Orias laughed again, more jovially this time, as lightning lanced
the ground, and its thunderous rumble shook the earth.
He was unphased by all the commotion, and he held up a silver
chalice to the sky, offering a prayer with some utterances about
the sacrificial spirits, using a tiny ladle to dip and sprinkle the
contents all around the area.

But the ground shook fiercely and knocked him out of balance, which startled him at first, but then he smiled again and uttered, "Let us take the precautions before larger movements arrive."

So, his team swung into action and began to dig the water well with incredible speed.

Amdusias and his men helped by directing traffic and assisting wherever possible. They all had a heightened sense of alarm, as if something catastrophic was about to happen unless they could take the necessary precautions, yet they were also excited by the optimism of their leaders and hopeful for the rewards.

Some of them laid plans for the groundwork while others formed an assembly line from a nearby quarry to the main work site. And others dug down with specialized tools to hollow out the well and other foundational pits. Some were assembling boats, others prepared rope and netting and mortar, and blacksmiths fashioned hammers and rings to use with these assemblies.

Amdusias and his people had some fishing boats in service, which they used to catch fish and feed the hungry workers.

There were several accidents and failures along the way, as they built multiple large sea-faring vessels. The ballast on one of the vessels was weak and snapped like a twig, causing injuries and a general outcry due to the calamity, which led to some dissension and murmuring from Orias' legion of strong workers.
They momentum stopped and they nearly lost the faith amidst the uproar, and they complained bitterly, proclaiming that this project was a lost cause, doomed from the start.

But Orias was steadfast and uplifted his troops. He admitted that this calamity was a disaster beyond repair, but the overall cause was not lost. So, the men regained their optimism and carried on with the work.

An adversary was roaming in disguise among all the commotion, totally undetected due to the intensity of the work, with so many teams working in constant motion all around each other.

He had secretly sabotaged the mast to cause the calamity, hoping to destroy the will of the workers and thwart the plans of Orias.

And seeing that Orias uplifted his troops despite the calamity, the saboteur tried to stir up contention and doubt in other ways. He approached Orias and tempted him, with simple flattery and cunning language, asking him to enter into a trade agreement with a nearby civilization. He claimed they could increase their efficiency and open new lines of business and opportunities.

But Amdusias watched and knew something was out of order, sensing that Orias was uncomfortable with this trade proposal. So, he waited until the secret adversary left, then approached Orias to discuss.

"No worries, Amdusias. I declined the offer from this impostor, and we will continue to focus our honest craft."

"But Orias, if you know he is an impostor, why won't you take action to eliminate him from your ranks, and restore order?"

"Be patient, my dear Amdusias. We may be able to establish a mutually beneficial agreement with this man by playing along with his own game. We have the advantage because we can detect his lies and we know of his deceit. I will ask my first officer to watch him carefully and assign him to some menial tasks where he can't cause any serious trouble."

Orias paused, then continued, "Eventually I intend to use our leverage and arrange a deal with this man. Perhaps he will redeem himself and prove to be a useful ally."

"You have quite the nerve," responded Amdusias with doubts. "Your strategy is questionable, but I will follow along for now. However, I will watch the impostor closely, as I am not so trusting and forgiving as you."

"I agree that caution is in order," replied Orias, "so with your permission I want to adopt some new laws and regulations to prevent and eliminate similar accidents from...."

Amdusias liked the idea and cut him off mid-sentence. "That sounds like a fine idea. I will assign a team from among my ranks to serve as judges, with other officials to supervise and keep the system in check."

It was the first time Amdusias asserted himself in this effort. Orias paused, nodded his head in agreement, and finally added, "I trust you will include some of my people in the proceedings, for the sake of fairness...?"

Amdusias agreed.

And Orias thanked him, expressed gratitude, and promised to cultivate his virtues, develop his talents, and examine his faults.

Amdusias never had any reason to doubt Orias's resolve, so he wondered why Orias felt the need to offer these reassurances. "Who is he trying to convince?" he wondered, but he nodded along in agreement and felt good about the arrangement overall.

The saboteur made his way back to his makeshift shelter in the busiest section of the sprawling city, nestled in an alley amidst some vendors and merchants, masquerading as a homeless man in the dumps. And then, in an instant, after entering a small tent, he transformed into a miniature dragonfly of sorts, and flew off into the nearby mountainous desert lands.

The dragonfly entered through a rocky crevice in the mountain of Haaiah, off the beaten path, and into a large cavern where hordes of similar creatures buzzed around busily, engaged in various tasks to prepare for the oncoming cold season
Some gathered and preserved food, others built sturdy shelters, and other larger beasts were involved with engineering efforts to bolster their fortresses and defensive troops around the borders.

Upon entering the court, the saboteur approached the center area, which was ornate and beautifully decorated in a regal style.

The court was attended by twenty-nine other dragonfly creatures, all of whom were seated around a large oval table, eating and conversing over the day. He took his place, and the others were very interested to include him in the feast and the conversation, but before they had exchanged any niceties, a larger creature entered the area from behind a curtain, and all went silent.

An attendant announced the creature's presence with a low-pitched horn, then addressed him with a bow,

"Master Bune, how may we serve thee today?"

The three heads of Bune[3] were attached to his dragon-like body.

The first head was that of a canine, the second of a gryphon, and the third – in the middle – of a man. Each of the three heads moved independently and looked around in diverse directions to survey the room, and as he sat down the human head spoke in a high and comely voice, almost shrill yet somehow soothing to the nerves of all in the room.

"I have finished gathering the dead, and your new assignments are engraved upon the board," he said, referring to a large board on the northern wall of the room. The board had thousands of names listed in rows, written in tiny hieroglyphics, each of which with a corresponding location assigned. The room fluttered with gleeful whispers as the dragonflies rubbed their wings together to express their sustaining joy.

He spoke to the saboteur dragonfly directly, "I presume you have news for us here, so please do share with the assembly."

"Master Bune," he declared with some trepidation, "my attempt was a failure, but I am ready to try again. All I was able to bring back with me was this single bundle of golden thread."

He held up the bundle.

A startled silence filled the room for a long pause. Master Bune sighed as all three of his heads took on a sore disappointed look, each in perfect sync with the others. They looked up together as the human expressed his frustration with unintelligible whispers.

He then addressed all the council members in the room.

"This is disappointing news indeed, but not entirely unexpected. I suspected we would face difficulties. And now, we will need to change our strategy."

The council members listened attentively.

"There are troubling affairs in our kingdom, due to the foolish mistakes made by my father and others, and the kingdom is verging to complete ruin if we cannot find a way to gain leverage with the dwarves for the instrument we seek." Then he paused and held up the bundle of thread, and his human eyes widened. "Hmm. What do you know about this thread?"

"Master Bune," answered the saboteur, "I heard that it was spun by the demigod of the Mahashiah, called Marbas, and received by their orator and prophet, who goes by the name of Amdusias. I flew into his inner chamber and obtained the spindle secretly, my Lord."

The three heads of Bune lit up with delight, as he carefully held the spindle up to the light, staring at its glittering appearance. They smiled together and filled the room with a new hope. "Perhaps this thread will interest our neighbors to the south, and we can arrange a trade for our journey in exchange...."

"Our journey, Master?" one of the council members asked.

Bune had a special arrangement with the neighbors to the south, a competition of sorts, which he had set up between a few of the most promising inventors – a pair of brothers and their rival. These were amazing inventors, to say the least, as they had forged many peculiar tools and weapons, some of which had mysterious power. He suspected that they would covet this bundle of golden thread and compete to obtain it.

And sure enough, his next meeting with these inventors proved to be fruitful, as the competitors agreed to compete for the prize. They had already fashioned several renowned tools, such as the very hammer wielded by Samigina of the Ahlimiah, which was nearly indestructible and conductive, capable of channeling the wielder's energy to create thunderous movement in the air.

So, now they took upon them the task of creating two additional tools fit for the gods.

The team of brothers, known as Brash and Soren, set their minds on creating a new ring, while the other engineer, called Devin, set his mind upon forging a new spear tip. Both of which would be endowed with special properties.

Bune kept the spearhead for himself, but he offered the ring to Orias in the seaport civilization, which was named Samigina in honor of the half-equine, half-human deity of the Aylimiah, who appeared to Amdusias and provided Orias to serve with him.

In doing so, Bune was able to establish a peaceful trading agreement with the seafaring and industrious civilization of Samigina and secure passage with them across the great waters to new lands of promise.

Meanwhile Samigina joined his place among the Ahlimian kingdom above, having redeemed his fallen state and gained an elevated status as a servant and probate of the angels. He remembered his divine heritage and celebrated with the angels.

[1] *Samigina*, anciently known as *Gamigin* according to Dr. Rudd, has more work to accomplish before he will gain salvation, and every night he wails and moans until he's weary, crying into his pillow until his eyes waste away and grow weak with sadness. The reader can research Gamigin in the various grimoires but suffice it to say that his fall was tragic, for his birthright and his heritage are of the most noble order. And yet his true destiny and his Higher Self, known as *Aylimiah* or *Allah*, is among the most important archetypes in the series, for he maintains balance and integrity among all the gods, giants, and dwarves.

Samigina is symbolized by the Master Mason of Freemasonry, who works mighty works and inspires others with good deeds. His breath is controlled, steady, and reassuring to all around him, and he helps those in need, such as those with mental troubles, those who need help identifying treachery, and those who need help in their voyages (especially at sea). He advises us to take great care and caution, which leads to success in industry, etc. And along with the mystical traditions, he teaches the tradition of responsibility and citizenship in a noble and honorable form, with justice and reason balanced by mercy.

He also preaches faith, but not blind faith; it must be based on some skepticism and intelligence, which allow true freedom and independence of personal thought, and accordingly, absolute responsibility and accountability for our thoughts and actions.

Reason and science are vital aspects of this faith, and so the Master spends much time at the trestle board using mathematics, geometry, and reason to draft his plans.

Yet, as Mr. Albert Pike wrote, *reason itself will eventually be "alarmed at the abysses" of infinity and creation, and therefore "it is silent and gives place to the faith it adores."*

Samigina eventually finds balance and returns to his completed and exalted self (Aylimiah) through the practice of pranayama, or yogic breathwork, in which he rediscovers the essential nature of thought (not merely whimsical "thought" but *real* thought). He finds that a *thought* of an intelligent existent force begets great acts and beingness. And he learns (or *remembers,* really) not only his heritage, but also his eternal identity and destiny.

On the surface, this remembrance comes through visions and revelations which he receives from his Father during times of extraordinary turmoil and distress, but also, on a long timeline, this involves coming to terms of love and understanding with his supernal mother אמא, the Great Sea, who has now transformed to אימא, the Great Productive Mother, who is far greater than מלכות (The Kingdom); that is: far greater than the "inferior" maternal bride queen (spouse of the forms).

Therefore, he recognizes that he is on the level and may freely communicate with the אלהים (Elohim), of the angelic order of אראלים (Aralim or Thrones) and even יהוה אלהים (JHVH Elohim), if he observes שבתאי (Sabbath, Saturn, or rest) and follows all the other commandments.

The dragon is furious with אימא because despite his efforts to use and manipulate her and her first child (and her future offspring) for his own personal gain, she is blessed and protected, safe from his idle threats. The ironic truth is that the dragon is frightened by the waters of the sea which he helped create in the beginning! So, the dragon stands to the side and waits, ofttimes wailing and moaning while she and Aylimiah thrive, along with those who keep the commandments of God and hold to the testimony.

[2] *Orias* or *Ooriax*, as he is known, has much to teach us about the eternal mind, by which we learn much (in fact *ALL*) about the body as well. He appears as lioness and rides upon a horse, whips his serpentine tail, and holds two hissing serpents in his right hand. He commands thirty legions and has vast knowledge of the physical universe, the stars, the planets, and their virtues, and he can bless men with favors from friends and foes alike, transforming them to greater wonders.

His higher calling is that of *Herahael*, who knows all things and always praises and observes His miracles, as often as possible. (Refer to the 113th Psalm of David.) He shows how to cultivate virtues and examine faults, realizing that we were all beggars.

Also known as *Ella*, he leads to success and provides treasures through books and the banking system. And just like Samigina, he is defined by movement and motion, yet with the assurance that things will be as they were, after the movement is gone by. Orias takes careful attention to measurements, and he ceases the foolish lies of the ego, letting go of all temporal things, realizing that they only last for a time and will be restored later.

From the rising of the sun to the setting, he praises God, restores families, and heals the barren womb. Life sprouts up amidst all the noise, and despite the temptations, he focuses on his craft.

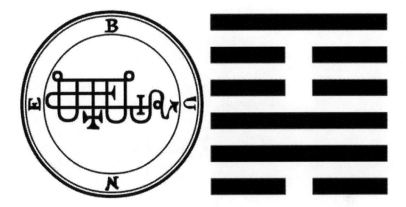

[3] *Bune* commands thirty legions and has a unique appearance, with three heads (dog, gryphon, and man) on his dragon body. His voice is distinctive as well, high and comely, and he uses it to gather the dead, assign them to locations, and communicate eloquently with man. He can provide riches and answers to a true man. His potential is profound if he will just remember his true higher eternal identity, which is *Haaiah* (hidden from view). This requires him to call out morning and eve, and all day long, to know his creator and uphold correct statutes and principles, to know and follow the commandments and the voice of God. (Refer to Psalms 119:145.)

Insomuch as he calls out daily in this manner, he will realize that there are "services to perform" (*kû*) due to troublous or spoiled affairs verging to ruin.

In a large degree these problems are due to the mistakes and false teaching of those who came before, such as his parents and earlier generations, but he must not allow these conditions to fester in him and cause even greater turmoil.

The proper quest in all this is to find and use the *instrument* fit for his work. In doing so he will receive praise, and he will see the path ahead more clearly, toward better days ahead. Some of the work is troublesome, yet rewarding with the proper attitude.

Chapter 4 – Charity

Foreword

And in the spirit of Samigina, we move along quickly in the story. In the previous chapter, I mentioned that successful pranayama breathwork requires asana, or posture, and now we will analyze the latter in greater detail, as provided by Vassago-Sytael.

Asana is "steady comfortable posture" (sthira sukham asanam), which is most desirable, and which allows Vassago to rise above dualities and meditate upon infinity (ananta samapattibhyam).

In the ancient Norse legends, the goddess Siff is renowned for her extraordinary beauty and her golden tresses, which covered her from head to foot like a brilliant veil. And Loki devised a plan to steal her beautiful hair, but Thor caught him afterwards, gripping him in the throat until he begged for forgiveness and swore to replace the hair.

So, Loki made a deal with a dwarf devil named Dvalin to reseed the hair, such that it would grow as luxuriantly as ever before.

And Siff, rather than fighting against her undesirable situation, focuses her mind and stays on the course with a steady and comfortable posture, choosing internal subjects to hold in mind, by which she finds magnificent strength, light, and might.

Some readers may see the parallel to Persephone-Proserpine, who maintained similar dignity and a positive attitude after she was ravaged by Pluto-Hades. And perhaps she wanted revenge, but she also knew the lies of the deceiver, who desires to split and possess the minds and bodies of those who give into the temptations of the flesh and wander in this temporal existence.

Siff is not only the goddess of the harvest, but also the mother of the great god of winter, known as Uller. She follows an annual cycle which defines this archetype, with its seasons ruled by the Sun, the Moon, and the Earth's revolutions upon her tilted axis. But despite all this movement, there is balance and stillness in each and every frame of reference, due to her great regularity, and a constant flow of time and gravity.

And as Peter writes, every day is as a thousand years in the end; every smaller cycle contained within the larger, and so on.

In the upcoming chapter, we meet Vassago, whose story and identity are parallel to that of Siff. Through careful posturing, she learns to meditate upon the Eternal and Infinite Creator, who wears the changing physical world as a garment, and who endows us with his blessings (see Psalms 102).

And through this meditation, Vassago finds and maintains her higher identity, who is known as Sytael.

Sytael and Siff exemplify how to embrace the light, which is obtained through steady and comfortable posturing and sincere prayer, along with all the manifestations of the Briatic world, which is the sphere of the creations.

They embrace the light through affinity, kinship, and reverence.

Their words are few, yet they honor their promises and plights with perfect sincerity and integrity, which allows them to thrive in the brightness.

In the lands of Mahashiah, the raven-headed

Andras of Anyael, former king of the realm, continued to lead his people with help from his friends, Andrealphus of Damabyah and Glasya-Labolas of the Nith-Hayach, with their many legions. And they prospered in the land.

Amdusias of the Aychael had previously expelled Andras from the kingdom and stripped his title as king, yet Andras had taken on the mantle of a king in this new land, in his own right.

And Amdusias continued to search for a new high king to anoint, but he was also keenly interested in the progress of Andras and vowed to assist him in a journey across the great waters.

So, he sought out and enlisted the support of Orias of Herahael and Bune of Haaiah, who both serve Samigina of the Aylimiah.

They were motivated for different selfish reasons, but they came to an agreement and offered to assist in the journey.

Reconciliation would not come easily, as Amdusias and Andras were not yet on speaking terms, so any diplomatic arrangements would be difficult. Amdusias was intrigued by the civilization and the resourcefulness of Andras, and he gained more respect for him as he continued to observe. He remembered that Marbas had plans for Andras to lead a new movement across the waters, and he commanded that they work as a team to ensure success. But how would it happen?
Amdusias was able to remotely view the land, but he would surely be arrested if he tried to enter uninvited, without disguise.

Time was of the essence, so he couldn't afford the risk of being caged and forced to beg for mercy and a meeting with Andreas. There must be another way, he thought.

So Amdusias made camp for the night in the woodlands outside the eastern border of Mahashiah to seek counsel from his God and consider his next steps.

And as he prayed, he felt a new presence.

He opened his eyes and beheld a cloud of tiny glowing entities, sparkling in the surrounding air, fluttering around in rhythmic waves like a whirlwind of glowflies, each with its own tiny light, yet somehow interconnected as a whole entity with a hive-mind.

But it whispered off into the distance, leaving him to wonder what it all meant.

Several minutes passed. And while pondering on this strange occurrence, he looked down and watched a crab-like creature scuttle across the ground, quickly at first, but then more slowly, and finally turning to approach him, with pincers and tentacles actively sensing the surroundings while he observed.

"What is this?" he wondered aloud.

The creature moved quickly again, this time startling Amdusias so that he reacted with a flip of his foot, and accidentally kicked it directly into the hot burning coals of the campfire.

But the creature seemed unphased and crawled across the scintillating flames without acting surprised, emerging with excellent posture, now glowing as if it absorbed some of the energy from the flames.

Out in the woods, other similar creatures emerged from the dark, twenty-six in total, with strong shells protecting their vitals, glowing warmly from within, while they hummed a soothing tune together. They seemed very comfortable, fearing nothing, and offering peace.

Amdusias trusted their approach as he noticed their intrinsic beauty and their light movements, and he introduced himself.

"Hello there, brilliant friends. I am Amdusias of the Aychael, most sincere and pious in my quest to serve and acquire wisdom. How may I call thee?"

There was no audible answer, but as Amdusias was sensitive to psychic projections, he quickly realized that these beings were telepathic like himself, and the leader of these beings – the one who emerged from the fire – was communicating telepathically, directly into his mind with images.

At first, the images came flooding in with such a torrent that he couldn't assemble any specific meaning, but then they took turns, modulating the communication and settling into a comfortable highly-structured telepathic connection, sending images and words back and forth with fluency.

"Vassago of Sytael," the creature projected his name in perfectly audible form within Amdusias' mind.
This simple-looking creature was obviously far more complex and intelligent than Amdusias had originally supposed.

"Have you lost something?" it asked.

Then it shared a visual layout of the entire landscape for miles, along with a flood of information about the territory.

Amdusias sat down, somewhat perplexed, and felt grateful for this kind offering of knowledge.

Vassago[1] invited Amdusias to assume a comfortable posture and rise above the "dualities" by meditating upon infinity and the eternal nature of God, who wears the world as a garment.

"What an honor!" Amdusias proclaimed. Then he went silent and tried to accept the invitation with an open mind and heart. He knew that Vassago wanted to help him find hope and refuge, and to recognize and thank the Lord. His heart was filled with joy and gladness as they began to sing praise in their psychic silent chorus, recounting all the wonderful works of creation.

There was a gentle humming audible in the material realm, but the true and most glorious expression of their choir was only visible and audible in the psychic, beyond words to describe. And yet, along with the psychic sense also came an enhanced sense of physical reality, which seemed brighter and more vivid.

Suddenly, Amdusias recognized his close kinship to Vassago, and identified with the hard-shelled, armored creatures around the world. He thought of his primal existence in the dim past, and imagined himself with a shelled belly of sorts, a primitive gastropod or tortoise-crab, living inside and learning from the trees which provided shelter within their hollows. Then he saw himself emerging from the hollows carefully, often returning for safety, and building strong armor to protect against the elements. He felt his own chain-mail armor and wandered off in wonders.

Vassago then transformed from the crab-like entity into an extraordinarily beautiful angel, covered from head to foot with her long golden hair, which shimmered with a brilliant luster whenever she moved, and draped like a veil from her head down to her feet. She transmitted to Amdusias that she was none other than the goddess of the harvest, and the mother of winter.

She motioned upward and Amdusias beheld a brilliant-white stock dove above, descending upon them in a gentle fall.

"This is my son Malthus," she showed. "He will help you, and you will help him."

In this instant, as the dove descended, Amdusias realized there was something very special and peculiar about the dove, for a tide of spiritual awareness swept over his body and mind, and he felt lighter and even brighter than before, clearly endowed with a gift by merely being in the presence of this new entity whom she had called Malthus[2]. He felt a sudden urge to kneel, show his reverence, and prepare to learn and work.

Vassago and his followers scurried with a graceful elegance, then joined together in a blinding bright light, which grew brighter as each being joined the sphere, until they were all assembled as a brilliant globe, floating in the air.

And then they disappeared.

But the dove Malthus remained, and transformed into a man, dressed in high regalia like a decorated earl. And he introduced himself in a hoarse voice. "I am Malthus Agla, fallen from the Haymaiah, eager to return. My journey brings me to this place, and I trust we can help each other."

Amdusias was overjoyed and humbled by his kind offer, but then he noticed that Malthus stumbled a bit, took a few clumsy steps, and looked around in a daze of confusion before tumbling and crashing to the ground with a thud.

"Are you alright?" he asked, stepping forward to offer his hand.

"Oh!" proclaimed Malthus, obviously flustered and embarrassed as he stood up and brushed the dust from his uniform. "I'm quite all right. This is just the first time I've assumed physical form in this realm. Pardon me."

But the embarrassment of the fall seemed to build up with each passing moment, as he treaded carefully to avoid yet another fall. His face turned hollow and menacing, as if he was struggling with internal pain, and an unquenchable fire burned brightly in his eyes. Amdusias worried that he might explode with rage.

But thankfully, over the next few minutes he held his composure, and they both began to rest easy once again.
It occurred to Amdusias that this decorated creature, seemingly so genteel and polished on the surface, was capable of intense

wrath and mighty destruction if he were provoked. He carried a depth of sorrow and emptiness within his soul, which manifested in his demeanor as a mixture of solitude and strength.

Amdusias realized he had failed to introduce himself.

"Malthus Alga, I am called Amdusias of Aychael. Welcome."

"Amdusias of Aychael, I am at your service," replied Malthus in a gruff voice. He looked around the camp site, then looked back at Amdusias and continued, "I may not be the strongest among your servants, but I am strict, and I adhere to my integrity."

Amdusias was taken aback by his humble approach.

"Your brightness is stunning, Malthus Alga, and I appreciate your kind offering. I anticipate we can work together nicely toward free course and success."

They continued to talk and took camp for the night, resting and exchanging ideas about how they would enter the neighboring lands of Mahashiah to enter negotiations with Andras.

".... There is another intelligent being, a mighty prince with twenty legions, protective and loyal, knowledgeable about the deep questions of all creation, and a strong loyal friend of mine. He is called Orobas. I believe we should seek his help."

"Okay Malthus, but timing is of the essence. My command...."

"I understand, Amdusias," interrupted Malthus. "We should be able to locate him in the nearby prairies, where he dwells."

With little further discussion, the two agreed to seek Orobas[3], dismantled their camp, and headed into the northeastern territory.

As the two journeyed, they heard a strange and pitiful cry echoing from a valley:

"Waaaaaaaaahhhhhhhhhhhh-hrrrrrrrrrrrr-hrrrrr!!"

They followed the cry and came upon a small horse-like beast, trapped under a wood carriage, which had somehow toppled upon the benighted creature. He flailed his three free legs up in the air, grimacing and moaning, not because he was wounded, but rather because his pride was injured. His bare butt bounced around as he squirmed to break free, but he only lodged himself even more deeply underneath the wooden structure, which had metal trappings and other adornments to weigh him down.

"What have we here?" asked Amdusias, somewhat amused.

"Save me!" screeched the horseling, "I am dying!!! Hrrrrrr!!"

Then, just out of view, something rustled in the brush, and they paused to determine who was coming. Amdusias feared a trap. But, proceeding slowly from the brush, a much larger horse emerged and chuckled under his breath, then paused to identify the strangers. "Ah, Malthus. Please excuse me while I assist my young friend here."

"No problem, Orobas!" replied Malthus, with a sideways glance to Amdusias, beaming with gladness as they found the prince. "May we help? My senior companion here is called Amdusias."

"No need, but thank you. This is a common accident for the young ones," replied Orobas with some stress in his voice, seemingly identifying with the young one as if he had been through this himself.

Amdusias was pleased to see that Orobas was another horse, since he was fond of the equine race and form. He felt kinship.

Orobas moved forward to free his young friend, and he realized the situation was worse than he suspected. The young horse had managed to wedge the hull of the carriage beneath the stump of an uprooted tree.

The only apparent solution was to dismantle the carriage, so he whistled for a team of young attendants, who came running in scarlet aprons to assist the prince. He ordered them to remove the wheels and front piece of the carriage, and after discussing among themselves briefly, they proceeded to make some cuts and create an opening for the captive.

As night was falling, Malthus was glad to project light upon the work area so everybody could see clearly.

Orobas was satisfied with his team, despite their leisurely pace.

Amdusias and Malthus assisted as the little horse broke free and made his final escape, limping off with only a few cuts and a bruise on his hind-left leg, and a bruised ego.

"Now let this be a lesson to you, young one," boomed Orobas, standing up to his full height – a mighty stallion indeed.

The little one nodded and scampered off into the nearby trees, and the attendants followed, leaving the three leaders to discuss, with carriage parts strewn around the ground in front of them.

"Have you found your wife yet, Orobas?" asked Malthus, innocently enough yet somewhat foolishly, not realizing it was a sensitive subject.

Orobas didn't answer directly but shook his head.

Malthus realized his error and tried to change to another subject.

"Well, that is unfortunate indeed, old friend. I hope you find one very soon, but in the meantime, we have another matter to ask you about if you're willing to discuss."

"Go on," responded Orobas. "There is only one path forward in this world, and I suspect our meeting is not mere coincidence."

His tone was extremely deep and serious, with an unshakable sense of stability in his presence. He kept a steady posture, which reminded Malthus of Vassago, as he walked unscathed upon the scintillating flames.

Malthus and Amdusias took turns explaining their predicament and plans, and Orobas heard everything they said, but cared very little for the various details. His mind was more interested in the eternal scheme of things, so he seemed aloof and disinterested.

"Orobas? Are you listening?"

"Hmm? Oh, yes," he replied. "When do we leave?"

They all exchanged glances, and Amdusias was feeling uneasy about the exchange.

"Well, Orobas, didn't you understand our concern with...."

"Please, yes, yes," he interrupted, mildly annoyed with the delay. "I understand and I think you're wasting effort talking about it, giving place for the lies of the deceiver to wander aimlessly in your split minds."

They stood speechless, and then Orobas continued cryptically, "The Earth moves through the seasons as she spins on her axis and revolves about the Sun, yet she maintains perfect balance. Now is the time to use the momentum we have been given and exert ourselves to...."

He stopped himself, then stared directly at Amdusias and said, "Surely a visionary like yourself, Amdusias, can see that the Lord of All is on our side?"

Amdusias cleared his throat, then answered, "Oh yes, Orobas. You are right, and I confess that I had lost myself in the details, and I forgot to seek guidance. Thank you for your words and your sense of clarity."

Malthus smiled and added, "This is why I knew we would need your help, dear Orobas. Your presence of mind is magnificent, and your strength will inspire us and many more to action."

Orobas shrugged off the compliment and asserted himself again. "We need not fear what any creature can do. Let us tune into the eternal plan with faith and adorn our lives with good actions."

So, they set off into the golden fields, which were ripe and ready for the harvest. Their goal was to confront the border together and enter peace talks and other negotiations with the Mahashiah.

And, as they journeyed together, Malthus and Amdusias thought about Vassago with her beautiful hair and brilliant light, and they described the experience in detail to Orobas.

Orobas smiled knowingly.

"Vassago understands the flames and can co-exist with them, along with the *Cheshalim* – the Burning Ones – because she and others like her allow the flame and heat to purify and enlighten the body and mind like a refiner's fire. The flames generate new life for those who can withstand and survive, and such is the resurrection of all life."

He spoke loudly and boldly, so that almost the entire entourage could hear him. They listened intently and drew strength for an upcoming battle if required.

Malthus plucked a single grain from the field and stuck it in his pack as a reminder of this great truth. Perhaps he would need a memento to help him remember in the future when the inevitable challenges arise.

They journeyed a few miles until the sun began to set, and it was time to make camp. They set about their duties and preparations for the evening.

The morning had barely arrived, and the Sun was still behind the eastern mountains, barely lighting the sky, as a panicked horse came rushing up and woke them all with his panting.

"Sir!" he exclaimed to Orobas. "We have been attacked!!"

Orobas asked him to calm himself and explain the situation in more detail.
"The attack was unprovoked and without honor, Lord Orobas. Three of our fellow workers, Horana, Dogatha, and Elianoran, never returned after gathering and chopping wood yesterday. We found Elianoran, who escaped with serious injuries and is now unconscious, but his two brothers are dead."

The messenger paused while Orobas and the others looked on, then continued, "They were ambushed and slaughtered near the Mahashiah border, but we were unable to locate or identify any of the assailants. Elianoran claimed the attackers were cloaked, and they approached in the darkness, and one of them used some sort of scythe to deliver the death blows."

Orobas stood in somber dismay but stood firmly.

"Orderly, have you taken care of the bodies?" asked Orobas.

"Yes sir, they are presently in the mortuary, awaiting final rites. Shall I inform the families sir?"

"Thank you, but no. Let me learn more and handle this myself."

Malthus held the single golden grain which he had picked from the field in his hand. He lifted his posture gently and twisted the grain gently as he peered at it, then looked upwards and sighed.

He had hoped this moment wouldn't arrive so quickly.

At the funeral services for the two fallen scouts, Orobas spoke few words, but the words he spoke were poignant and powerful. He called upon God to reveal the allegories and secrets of this new passage, not only the passage from this life into the afterlife, but also the passage of the survivors into new lands.

".... Help us to understand our duties and obligations in this life, dear Lord of the Heavens. Amen."

And Malthus added a few words as well. He didn't know the fallen scouts, but he admired their heroic courage – their faith and steady composure even in the face of danger, to fulfill the will of the Lord. He invoked the Spirit with powerful words, with sincerity as few had heard before.

"There will be more danger ahead but let us keep our wits close. Let us remain calm, comfortable, and steady, trusting the Lord and his angels to prepare the way."

As Malthus spoke, they all felt the warmth and witnessed the light of the Lord descending upon them, the invisible presence of Vassago in their midst.

Vassago oversaw these proceedings and inspired proper words.

She understood the vital importance of words in a time like this.

Amdusias recalled the inscription which hung upon the wall in his childhood home, which read,

"Letters are more powerful and capable than ships
As vessels to carry riches from place to place." --Unknown

[1] Here we have *Vassago*, overseeing twenty-six legions of spirits. She is a mighty princess who assists in the discovery of things that have been lost or hidden, and she declares what she knows with a good nature, inspiring hope even in the gall of despair.

At first, she may seem like a simple-minded creature, especially when compared to the dramatics of all the others, but she is quite complex and extremely intelligent, tempered by moderation and self-control, so she is stunningly beautiful and well-liked.

Her posture is excellent, and she withstands the hot scintillating flames without harm. Her mild manners and appearance allow her to communicate well with creatures, who trust her approach. Her higher identity is that of *Sytael*, a great protector who will oblige those in need of her service.

She seeks to provide hope and refuge for others.

The trigrammatic representation here is *lî*, which is signified by fire, lightning, and the Sun, which are emblems or manifestations of that brightness. And the implements of battle, such as armor shining brilliantly, buff coats, helmets, spear tips, and swords, are also reflective of that brightness when used well in justice. And in nature, we see the same dynamic in the hard-shelled animals like turtles, crabs, spiral univalves, mussels, tortoises, and hollow (often rotten) trees, ripe as fuel for the fire.

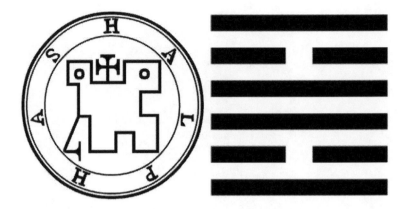

[2] The double-*li* representative it is known as *Malthus* or *Halphus*, who engages his twenty-six legions to build towers of defense, manufacture ammunition and weapons, and deploy warrior units. He is a great Earl who speaks with a hoarse voice and appears as a stock dove, still close to the Holy Spirit despite his fallen state. His real identity is *Haymaiah*, who is nicknamed *Agla*.

Haymaiah knows and reveals the secret place of the Most High, wherein the promise exists for protection, refuge, and a long life. With this awareness he can identify fraud, threatening weapons, evil beasts, and infernal spirits. He is "the triune and the one", the hope of all children of the earth, and the governor of all that relates to God, which leads to treasures on heaven and earth.

His will is as one with the Most Holy, in the most intimate sense.

He retains this intimacy due to his dutiful adherence to what is correct in the most docile and humble way.

He acts with obedience, kindness, and servitude, burning bright as he fulfills his tasks, endowed with special power to transform all under the sky to light and perfection. The universe sees his influence and obedience toward health and beauty of the whole, so it loves him and provides for his needs.

The brightness of Malthus is the very essence of intelligence, and the core of all the created universe, the seat of the soul.

Malthus is not without weaknesses. For within his strong shell, he is docile and vulnerable like a cow, more docile than the ox, and able to act in strict obedience and adherence to the rules. And the result of this strict obedience is a stunning brightness, which leads to free course, success, firmness, and correctness. His tears flow in torrents as he groans and the cycle continues, yet no criminal can resist his burns, just as no darkness can repel his light. His prayer is a similitude to the 102nd Psalm of David.

[3] *Orobas* is a mighty prince with twenty legions, who appears as a horse, very loyal and protective, knowledgeable about the past, present, and future, knowing all about the creation of the world.

He bestows various honors and restores friendship among foes, and otherwise strengthens friendships.

His nature is such that he prefers to move in one direction, but he must face up to various challenges and obstacles in his life which inhibit that movement, leaving him feeling trapped and enclosed, like a tree unable to spread its branches.

The journey is long and slow, characterized by some limiting factors which impede his progress.

He begins to doubt his own instincts because he put his faith in a specific tree, not realizing it was a stump and would not thrive, so he became trapped, and he prolonged the problem with his own stubbornness and stupidity, for a period of many dark years.

But eventually, he comes to understand that complaining or pleading will avail him very little or nothing, so he remains master of himself and prepares his mind to sacrifice all to accomplish his singular purpose.

The stress and pressure (straightening) have an empowering effect on him as he buckles down and moves along the path, accepting that he cannot please everybody along that path.

He realizes that he would rather endure the stress with honesty and uprightness rather than slip back into stupid ways, and he realizes that actions, not words, would be required to succeed.

Whereas before he worried about the defiles of water all around, he now decides to build above the dry marsh and allow the water to flow underneath (*khwăn*).

As a result of his dedication, discipline, and principle-based approach to accomplish his singular purpose, he sacrifices his old ineffective habits and self-deluding lies which promulgated those poor behaviors. And so, he remembers and reconnects with his eternal identity and his highest final form, *Mabahayah*, who governs morality and religion, distinguished by his good deeds and piety.

He responds most readily to the sincere request of those in need of comfort, consolation, or compensation, especially children.

Chapter 5 – Severity

Foreword

Now we will meet Valefor, who became known in the Norse legends as the god Frey, the son of Njord, who inherited the kingdom of the light elves when he lost his first tooth. The Aesir were very welcoming, even loving and accommodating to Frey and his sister Freya after the hostage trade, so this Vanir lord became part of the family and coexisted in peace and harmony.

The gods favored this lord of the sunlight and summer showers, gifting him with a magical sword and a ship, and Gullinbursti. The elves and fairies obeyed his will. But Frey fell from grace when he climbed Odin's throne and cast his gaze upon the fair giantess maiden Gerda, becoming possessed with desperate feelings for her, willing to manipulate and steal her love with bribes and ultimately a threat, delivered by his best friend.

It's taken some time, but Valefor-Frey eventually found a way to redeem himself and keep himself busy, even somewhat happy, during the cold of winter when she isolates herself and he rides his chariot alone. This mighty duke, who used to bellow in pain as a lion with the head of an ass, now laughs with mirth and distributes gifts during the Christmas ride, with ten legions to pull his chariot and assist, and we commemorate with the yule (wheel) traditions of bringing fire and light to the season.

He still enjoys his rides atop his golden-bristled boar or in the golden chariot, and he dashes through fire and water atop his powerful steed Blodughofi. And in favorable winds, he rides in his magic ship Skidbladnir for fun and adventure. He enjoys a life of constant travel, but he always returns to his homestead, where his temple, the house of God, resides permanently.

It is fitting that Frey's name is the northern synonym for "master" because he exemplifies the essence of the same, traveling to receive his masters' wages, always fair and honest, and so forth. R.B. Anderson said, "he causes not tears to maids or mothers: his desire is to loosen the fetters of those enchained, and he always puts on a great feast at the homestead".

While within his home, Gerda's brother Beli attacked Frey when he was without his legendary sword, and Frey snatched the stag antler from his wall to defend himself. It was not so much the specific tool or weapon he chose, but rather his noble intention and just cause under God, which decided the fate of this contest. As David writes, "the Lord is a stronghold for the oppressed, a stronghold in times of trouble.... He who avenges blood is mindful of them; He does not forget the cry of the afflicted."

Valefor practiced great concentration to reconnect with his original identity, which is known as Lelahael. The yogis would say that he practiced dharana, wherein the mind is bound to one place (desabandhah chittasya dharana), and the mind is trained to meditate through perseverance and by specific practice.

"Practice becomes firmly grounded when well-attended to for a long time without break and in all earnestness." –Unknown

The body follows the mind. The spine stands erect and elegant, blood surges where needed, the root or heart becomes strong, and the body is quickened by the spirit as if in distress or pain, but with deliberate continuity which overrides these sensations.

As Amdusias sat and wrote a letter to Andras,

while encamped in the green fields outside the land of Mahasiah, he paused to look at the candlelight and consider.

He assumed that he, together with Malthus and Orobas, and their hosts along with them, could carry out the mission to Mahashiah without any help. But his mind wandered to the city of Samigina. Should he call for recruits and reinforcements?

Amdusias was a spiritual leader over many provinces and cities, but he recently showed particular interest in the city Samigina. He was impressed by the leadership of Orias, the mighty mover and shaker who had the head of a lioness, the body of a horse, and a serpentine tail, with those two snakes to accompany him, and whose thunderous legions move quickly and powerfully.

Samigina was a thriving civilization now, even more so due to the partnership with Bune of Haaiah, that mighty and cunning dragon with three heads. They built ships and developed all sorts of industries to support and sustain the people, and they were blessed with excellent soil and crops, so they had enough food for their own people, storage for famines, and plenty more to export extensively. Various service-related industries and companies developed in the land, and a highway was built into the mountains of Haaiah, to strengthen their new partnership. Their borders were well-protected to protect the inhabitants, and the system of laws and courts was effective in identifying and resolving internal issues within the land.

So, the city of Samigina and the surrounding lands, and all their inhabitants, began to prosper in wealth, and they thrived with great happiness during this time.

Their wealth enabled them to import exotic goods, such as fine linens and beautiful fabrics, jewelry and precious metals, and other commodities to improve the richness and quality of life. The leaders created academic programs to educate their young, and social programs to support those in need of assistance with healthcare and other necessities of life.

The people began to separate into classes due to the social order, but they all met together weekly to worship as equals under God, realizing they all needed help. Amdusias was proud of Samigina and the Ahlimian overlords who watched over this great city.

Bune never confessed his prior conspiracy to spy in the lands and steal the bundle of golden thread, so this became a misery and a curse in the land, which developed due to his dishonesty and secrecy on the matter. He wielded the special spear tip, which greatly increased the strength and determination of his troops and workers, for it was said that he who possessed this spear tip could not lose in battle.

And Orias wore the enchanted ring, which was said to ensure fertility in the surrounding land and to guarantee an abundance of vegetables and fruits in the resulting crops. This ring had the curious ability to divide and reproduce itself once per year!

(Orias kept the duplicate rings safely guarded in the most central temple of the city, in a vault with the other sacred relics.)

Amdusias knew that the warriors of Bune and Orias would greatly increase their power and force, ensuring the success of the mission in Mahashiah. And he preferred to use a kinder and gentler approach, but the recent murder of two scouts in the open fields was alarming, so he prayed for guidance.

Indeed, the mighty canine-gryphon warriors of the Nith-Hayach, which were led by the fearsome Glasya-Labolas, were guarding the lands round about their capitol Mahashiah. And some were quick to react and attack without reasoning, so Amdusias feared that a sudden encounter might provoke unnecessary assumptions or attacks from either side, since his own people were still very angry about the deadly attack in the field.

So, Amdusias considered all these facts and prayed for guidance.

And the answer came to travel north and send for a contingent of Haaiahan warriors to bolster their forces and protect the pathway back to the city, and to patrol the fields near Mahashiah.

Therefore, he sent for reinforcements, and he informed the others that the will of the Lord was to travel north in small groups, staying close enough in proximity to communicate quickly from one group to the next, only a few hours apart.

He assumed that the goal was to encircle upwards and around the land of Mahashiah, then proceed through a northeastern passage. But he did not know the entire plan of his Lord, so he trusted only the direction to travel north, and he sent for reinforcements. It was enough to receive just one specific direction for the day.

He reminded his people that the Nith-Hayach have never fought with scythe weapons, nor used them as tools in the field, so it was unwise to assume that the murders of their compatriots were executed by the Nith-Hayach.

———————————————————————————

At nightfall, a chill spread over the land and froze the ground.

And the cold weather caused a few aches and pains during the day as they trekked northward around a ridge.

So, they traveled for three days in these terrible conditions, setting up makeshift camps for refuge. And on the fourth day, Amdusias wandered off at night to pray in a hidden cove and seek further counsel.

Meanwhile, in the lands of Mahashiah, Andras the Ravenhead and the others were deeply concerned by a recent series of thefts in the heart of the city.

"It must have been invaders from the south, sent by Amdusias," proclaimed Glasya-Labolas, with a foreboding grimace on his canine-like face. He shook his fist in fury, and his wings flexed as he spoke.

Seemingly bewildered and lost in thought, Aldrealphus paused, then shook his head wildly and replied, "No sir, this does not seem to be correct." He had assumed a human form for now, yet his hair shimmered with peacock iridescence.

"And how would you know? Your predictions are questionable at best lately," growled Glasya.

Andras sighed with a slight whistle through his raven beak, then interjected to prevent further debate.

"Let's be reasonable and work through this, men. We've made it thus far and we won't lose our focus...."

"This is an outrage!" exclaimed Glasya, his anger growing hotter by the moment. "What proof do you need? The central treasury has been robbed! We've searched every suspect in the land, and we embarrassed ourselves. This isn't an internal affair!"

"I agree...," started Aldrealphus.

"Stay out of this, Andreal...," Glasya yelled, then caught himself and continued, "Wait, what did you...? You agree with me?"

"Yes, I agree with you, Glasya. This is not an internal affair, but I sense another being, someone unknown...."

"Probably sent by Amdusias!" interrupted Glasya.

"It bellows in pain," continued Andrealphus, speaking directly to Andras now. "He is in the north."

Andras nodded. "Glasya, I know you are concerned about this, as we all are, and I assure you that I am also deeply committed to get to the bottom of this. Please, I need you to be patient, and I need your help to investigate further."

Then he turned to Andrealphus and inquired further about this bellowing he heard. "Up in the north? How did you learn this?"

"I have my ways, Master Andras. Surely you have some confidence in my intelligence network and...."

"Yes, yes, I do," Andras spoke with impatience. "I'd like to know the details and send a team to investigate further. In fact, I think we should embark on this mission together, all three of us now, along with a small cohort."

Amdusias continued in prayer, but was interrupted and aroused by the forlorn noises of a creature in distress in the distance.

"Who goes there?"

There was no response, but Amdusias approached the source of the intermittent sounds, which echoed from a nearby cavern. And as he drew closer to the source, he realized it sounded like the sobs of a child, but from a grown man, bellowing in dreadful pain without any regard for his surroundings, seemingly unaware or not caring that others could hear.

"May I help you?" asked Amdusias, upon seeing the lion-like creature sprawled out on his side, sobbing, totally limp from apparent exhaustion.

The creature was inconsolable for a while, but Amdusias was persistent and gentle with his approach, so eventually it calmed down and seemed to regain its composure to some degree.

His breathing mellowed out and he began to speak.

"How could I fall so far?" he started. "I've lost... I've lost it all."

"Pardon me if I am intruding in your personal affairs, good sir, but I have been sent to these lands by my Lord, and I suspect that our meeting is not merely a coincidence. I am known as Amdusias of the Aychael. May I... know your name?"

Amdusias was distracted as he spoke, and he looked off to try to identify some flashes of light in the nearby trees.

"It is quite all right, Amdusias of the Aychael. I apologize for my embarrassing display of emotion. My name is Valefor."

Amdusias noticed an impressive and flashy sword at his side, while a massive boar with golden bristles meandered up and nestled itself against Valefor[1], apparently hoping its presence would be unnoticed.

Valefor was apparently drunk with strong wine or guilt, or both, and he was ready to bear his soul and confess to this stranger. "I've committed a terrible sin, Amdusias."

"Go on, Valefor. Perhaps it would ease your soul to share the burden with me. I will not condemn you, and maybe we can help each other."

Valefor explained glumly that he had lied and manipulated to steal the love of a young lady:

"It was a sad, terrible mistake! I was blinded by pathetic lust, and now I've lost everything I loved as punishment."

He continued to tell his sad story, for which he felt extraordinary shame and guilt. He had asked his best friend to enter the ice kingdom and manipulate the woman, first with bribes and ultimately with a threat, to secure her love. "She relented and joined me, and she promised to love me, and all was well!"

He paused as if lost in thought, then continued, "But of course, all was lost, and I was a fool to believe that I could have such a perfect maiden. I was Lord of the sunlight and summer showers, traveling the realm aboard my skyship, and we were destined to rule the world of light together! But...."

"But you lost her...," Amdusias prompted, as the boar grumbled and oinked.

"Yes, yes. I've fallen from grace and will never return. If only I had never climbed the forbidden mountain and cast my gaze upon her...."

The confessional continued as Amdusias helped him to his feet, and he brushed off his coat. Then they walked to a nearby brook where a golden chariot was parked in the snowpack. The winter had set in now, and ice crystals flew all around in the chilly air. Luckily, they each had hefty coats and hats to wear for additional insulation from the cold, while the boar, who led a pack of nine others to pull the chariot, seemed unaffected by the chill.

Valefor was encouraged by Amdusias's concern and friendship, and he offered to prepare a meal of thanksgiving for good will.

Amdusias accepted.

They traveled in the air, aboard this unique skyship drawn by flying boars, flying in a northerly direction for several hours, right through the middle of a blizzard. Amdusias was thrilled with the ride, and he was astonished by the strange lights in the air ahead, which he had never seen before in all his years. Where were they?

The light grew brighter, and the mood became somewhat cheery despite the cold. And as they descended to land, Amdusias saw a large flowing river below, cutting through the ice, passing into a large and brilliant village which lit up the area.

Upon landing, he was fascinated to realize that Valefor was the leader of this large colony of elvish creatures, who moved with sparkling trails of light, always smiling, and singing together. Where in the world were they?

The creatures were overwhelmed with bliss at the return of their lord Valefor. They all fell into order and bustled with energy as they waited for new orders.

Valefor's mood lightened. His pain was still there, still running in the background, but he was functional now and seemingly motivated to get back to work.

"Perhaps there is hope ahead, Amdusias, in the spring season. And for now, we have work to perform."

Then he turned his attention to the leader of the elves and gave instructions for their next set of projects. He was strict and exact in his instructions, clearly a perfectionist, with an emphasis on high quality in their workmanship.

The elves seemed eager and overjoyed to comply, with each new task to complete. They asked specific questions to clarify and make plans for their work, and he took the time to answer each question in turn. No detail was too small, but the elves seemed to respect his time, so they only asked important questions.

And, while issuing these orders, Valefor noticed a new pile of foreign treasures in the work area.

"And what is this?" inquired, pointing to the treasure.

"Ah, new treasures obtained from various diverse locations, Father Future," answered the principal elf. They weren't being used and had sat around idly for some time, so we procured them for our own tasks. Aren't they beautiful? Imagine...."

"Enough!" interrupted Valefor with impatience and frustration. "This is unacceptable. We will return the items."

Valefor realized all too well, of course, that it was his own fault for setting a poor example for the elves, so he felt terribly guilty. After all, he thought, he had been the first to steal, and his theft was the most heinous of all!

"I have set a poor example for you, my friends, and I apologize. I was selfish and foolish, and now we have this curse upon us, with a debt of servitude to repay for my wanton desires.

"I feared that all was lost, but my friend here has enlightened me to realize that we may still be redeemed, and all will be restored! But we have a great work to do, and we must be perfect in our honesty and charity."

The elves cheered loudly and immediately went back to work, dancing and singing praises as they worked, trusting his words with absolute faith, determined to fulfill the requisite tasks and receive their rewards in the spring, after working through the cold winter.

Valefor told Amdusias about his ancestry and his departure from the Lelahael, an ancient race of beings who had a special gift of creating light, which they give away freely to all the world to inspire the search for knowledge and to cure all sorts of disease. His hope was to rejoin them in their efforts, but he had been cut off from communication ever since he conspired to steal.

Suddenly, he lowered his head in distress and placed his hands on his head as if he were in pain, then grimaced with took a stern look upon his face and straightened up again.

"Valefor, are you alright?"

"No, no I'm not. I can sense the cries of the afflicted in all the lands all about, and their sincere desires."

"Hmm." Amdusias paused to consider and empathize with him. "That sounds like an amazing gift you have, and a heavy burden as well."

There was no response, so Amdusias looked around and couldn't help but marvel at the unique mixture of science and art in action all around them....

"I have failed to live up to my purpose, Amdusias, and I must continue to repent. These are perilous times, but with the leadership of our God we will yet survive."

Amdusias was impressed by Valefor's concentration and faith, despite all his various difficult sufferings.

They walked outside, and Valefor looked upward and made a peculiar birdcall in the air, and after a few moments had passed, a response came from afar off with a similar call.

"Ah yes. Let me introduce my friend here, my apprentice...."

A large reddish-purple bird swooped down from the north sky, and it landed upon the ground gracefully, carefully tucking in its large wings and walking forward.

Twenty more birds followed, each landing with equal grace.

"I couldn't find it, Valefor!" squawked the beast. "It's useless!"

"Ah, patience my friend Phenex," said Valefor. Then he paused and turned toward Amdusias to make proper introductions.

"Amdusias, meet Phenex[2] of Aniael, an excellent friend and uplifting companion after my own heart. Phenex, please meet Amdusias of Aychael, the mighty prophet and orator from the southern territories."

Then he resumed his conversation with Phenex. "Patience, my good friend. Remember our prime course...."

"Yes, yes, it's impossible. I can't bind the mind to just one place! You've taught me..."

"Breathe and center yourself, Phenex," interrupted Valefor with a wave of his hand. "Remember your heritage and your destiny."

"I just don't remember, Valefor! I've been trying to do this for over eight centuries now!"

"Stop," uttered Valefor under his breath, barely audible.

The phoenix stopped and composed himself, and then his demeanor changed, as if he woke up afresh, now submissive, ready to learn again.

"Let us feast, old friend! I haven't seen you since last year and would love to hear about your latest adventures and findings."

They all agreed heartily, then separated to rest and prepare.

The elves prepared a large simple feast in about thirty minutes, with earthenware cups and bowls, and baskets of rice to pass around the table. They were all hungry and eager to devour this filling food, and they felt grateful for the offering.

The phoenix offered a special bottle of spirits to share with them, as he told a tale of his travels and lessons learned.

"It was perilous, I tell you, the defile was horrid and narrow! But we persevered through the danger in all due earnestness, never pausing and ever persisting...."

His spine became erect and elegant, and blood surged through his body as he spoke eloquently like a poet.

"The distress was intense! Yet our bodies and our minds were quickened by the Spirit in the moment, so we forgot about the pain and focused on the goal, and we escaped with our lives!"

"My dear Phenex," interrupted Valefor, "I trust the Aniael are very interested in your journey, and they are excited for your eventual return to the Seventh Throne. Your perseverance and concentration are remarkable."

"Well, I've learned much, and I feel prepared for yet another mission now. But I warn you, please be cautious and avoid the central island. I am no stranger to perversity, as you well know, and I can tell you that the island is ruled by some evil force."

His specialty was to survey and gather information in new uncharted lands. His most recent mission was to learn about distant lands across the great waters, but he and his flock were caught in a massive storm and landed upon an unknown island in the waters, with strange phantom-like beasts and traps all over. He sought to perform a survey and learn more about the island, but he was overwhelmed, nearly captured by phantoms.

"I almost died again, Valefor, but I'm getting better at this!"

Phenex had the peculiar ability to burn and resurrect himself from the ashes, but he preferred to live a long life with a full set of memories intact. The cost of resurrection was to lose some of the clarity of the old memories, as if the past life were a dream, and to start fresh with a new set of nerves and fibers and sinews and so on. It was a wonderful gift, but his goal was to return to his kingdom, known as the Seventh Throne, within another four centuries hence, and he felt his best chance was to preserve his current soul and hone his mind with concentration, which he described as binding the mind to a single place with meditation and perseverance. He believed that if he could master this art of true concentration, he would be worthy of the Seventh Throne.

Valefor laughed and responded gleefully, "You know the drill, dear old Phenex! Practice..."

Phenex joined in chorus,

"Practice becomes firmly grounded when well attended to for a long time, without intermission and in all earnestness!"

They both laughed heartily, and Amdusias joined in the fun by proposing a toast. "To Phenex, who stays fully committed to the course no matter the challenges, and gives all the glory to God, whose face shines brightly with sincerity despite perilous times!"

Amdusias knew that meeting Phenex was an important part of the journey, and he felt inspired by his revelations about nature, the sciences, and the arts. Perhaps the information about the island of phantoms would be important?

Meanwhile, the party of Andras, Andrealphus, and Glasya-Labolas traveled northward into the snowcapped mountains, bordering the lands of Lelahael, approaching the realm of Valefor and the rest.

"Halt," came a deep and powerful voice from above, and they froze in their tracks, feeling terrified and outwitted as they looked around to determine the source.

A giant creature emerged from a cleft in the rocky mountainside, and it moved slowly toward them, barely detectable against the mountainous terrain due its camouflaged ornamentation.

It towered over the travelers and looked down upon them as if they were rodents, and it stood ready for battle with both arms outstretched and poised with perfect symmetry on either side of its main body and facial armor. There was a particular elegance and beauty to this monstrosity....

"Come with me," it commanded with a gentle yet serious tone, which carried additional weight due to the appearance of more than twenty similar guardians in the backdrop, equally equipped and clearly ready to arrest the travelers.

Andras noticed the giant's massive feet right in front of him, and he peered upward to appreciate the full size of the creature. Then he looked downward again to the feet, which supported its giant body with perfect balance. He was impressed, but he also surveyed quickly to identify any potential weaknesses.

"Before we follow, we wish to know your intentions. What may we call you?" said Andras.

"We will talk later," responded the giant. "For now, you will come with us."

The travelers knew that they were in a precarious situation and decided to comply for the moment. Glasya-Labolas growled, but Andras reassured him with a request to keep it civil for now.

They were escorted into the mountainside, where one cavern led into another, and finally they arrived in some sort of makeshift mountain temple. The guardian knocked with a special knock at a massive doorway, then negotiated their entry with a door tiler.

And inside the temple, stunning artwork and ice carvings adorned the walls and the walkways, and a dazzling fountain sprayed with a perfectly symmetry in the center of the main hall. A huge staircase at the far end of the hall led upwards toward an enormous door, with guards on either side. Soft, incandescent light from lamps with stained-glass shades illuminated the snow and ice throughout the cavern, creating a surreal and stunning visual effect in the air.

"It's absolutely beautiful in here," noticed Andrealphus with wide-open eyes.

One of the guardians wheeled out a cart, slowly and deliberately, then stopped and scanned the visitors with a spectral red light.

They were alarmed at first, but realized the scan was painless, so they sat motionless for several minutes while the test proceeded.

After the scan was complete, the principal guardian spoke at last, very slowly and methodically. "I am Forneus, and I represent the Aornael. Thank you for your compliance. You may leave."

"Master Forneus[3]," spoke Andras with whatever courage he could muster. He felt sure that after such a dramatic encounter, there must be more to discuss. "Thanks for releasing us, but...."

Andras was at a loss of words. He should have been relieved to be released from this interrogation, or whatever it was, but he felt an urge to stay and inquire more about these creatures and learn more about their ways. Perhaps they could form some sort of partnership, or at least learn about some of their fascinating technology and advanced sciences?

Forneus seemed to understand perfectly, and then he responded, "We know you are a temple-building people from the south, Andras of Anyael. We could teach you much about the proper garments, tokens, signs, and methods of true temple ritualism. You have done well to reproduce the temple, but you have lost the true meaning and symbolism of the ordinances."

Andras and the others were transfixed and astonished by their great knowledge, and they were desirous to learn more.

Forneus went on to explain that with proper preparations and with concentration, they would yet learn the will of the Highest Intelligences and communicate with the vehement fiery beings, known as the Burning Ones, who spoke in the ancient language of tongues.

Andras was fascinated and interested, but he was also worried that there may be a catch, or perhaps some deception involved. Did these giants intend to overtake their lands and somehow subjugate them?

"What are your conditions, Forneus?" asked Andras wisely, realizing that there must be something in it for these frost giants. "We are interested to learn more, but what is your price?"

Forneus laughed. "I doubt there is anything you can do for us, Andras. We share our knowledge with men who desire to know the truth, who walk in straight paths with perfect symmetry."

Andras and the others listened intently.

Then Forneus continued while looking off into the distance, "Our queen was deceived by an evil lord, further north. She was tricked and subdued by an impostor. We desire her safe return."

Andras paused, then nodded, and expressed his condolences for their tragic loss. Perhaps there was something they could do for the giants after all. "Join us in our quest," he politely offered to Forneus, "and we will unite efforts to find your missing maiden."

But Forneus refused to leave the mountains, and just like that, the meeting ended.

Andras and his band offered to return with news of importance, and they made their way out.

As they were leaving the kingdom of Forneus to rejoin the main passage and continue their travels north, one of the Nith-Hayach scouts came running up the path, panting and out of breath.

"Sir," he said, speaking to Glasya-Labolas, "we've lost troops in a skirmish with Haaiahan dragons to the east. It seems they are guarding key areas along the eastern territory, and the tensions have escalated. We destroyed several of their mighty dragons, but our troops are becoming frightened and vastly outnumbered. We came to a truce for the moment, and I have been asked to deliver this letter from the enemy."

He held up the letter, which was sealed with the distinctive stamp of Amdusias.

Glasya-Labolas looked at Andras and nodded toward the letter, so Andras retrieved the letter and broke the seal. He was about to read it, then stopped and took a breath, and said,

"Let us regroup and discuss plans in an hour."

The dead were gathered from the field in a solemn procession, and each side of the battle felt rage and hatred toward the other, despite the truce. The warriors on either side expected to resume their fighting soon, and they made preparations to bolster their forces and determination, but the leaders were more circumspect and tried to maintain the peace, even if only temporarily.

Andras, Andrealphus, and Glasya-Labolas privately discussed the letter, in which Amdusias begged for peace and harmony, and for an alliance to prepare for a seafaring journey to the west. The letter was obviously written before skirmishes had occurred, yet it acknowledged the tension that existed between their tribes, and it suggested a more cooperative approach, unified by a common purpose as directed by the Lord.

The three leaders agreed to sleep on the issue and reconvene in the morning to discuss.

Meanwhile, Valefor observed the situation from high above, riding in his golden skychariot, distraught with the knowledge that his actions provoked this dilemma, eager to make amends. He spent the night delivering gifts of food and medical supplies to both sides of the battle, with additional clothing and supplies.

[1] *Valefor* always knew instinctively that the Lord is just and looks out for his own. He trusts the Lord. He is a valiant spirit known in the eternities as *Lelahael*, who was a perfect master, until he became selfish and stole, due to an evil ambition that grew inside, provoking him to gain a fortune by illicit means, and tempting others to steal as well. Now he seeks to repair these unintentional side effects of his sins. He knows he has become the premier example of perfection and perfect mastery, so he must not only provide high quality workmanship, but also show fairness for those who cry in affliction or sincere desire; not only providing gifts to help console them but also avenging their pain where necessary. And, despite the jolly image that he portrays in public, Valefor is also a man whose spirit is defined by his profound concentration. (Reference *Psalms 9:12*).

Valefor-Lelahael has the unique gift to give light to the world, which inspires mankind to acquire knowledge and cure disease. And he governs some of the most important aspects of life, praiseworthy as he is himself, such as love, fame, science, arts, and fortune, which gives him his nickname אבגד, *Father Fortune*.

Lelahael is perfectly united in purpose with the Almighty God, just like all the divine emanations in their pure state. His trigram is *khân*, representing the flowing water which creates peril yet also survival along the hidden path, only seen by one who walks forward with elegance, flexible to curve and roll as the wheel.

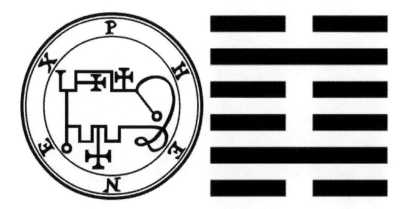

[2] *Phenex* is the extension of Valefor, and he is well known in modern lore as the Phoenix, who speaks and sings like a child, writes amazing poetry, and speaks about sciences if compelled. He governs twenty legions of spirits and has been known in the Seventh Throne as אניאל (*Aniael*), the identity which he finally embraced in this latter dispensation, after 1,200 years of penalty.

He now embodies a human form, which was his original form before the fall. He calls upon the name of the Lord God of Hosts with praise and gratitude, pleading for salvation as David does in the eightieth Psalm. He is fully committed to stay on the course, no matter which challenges arise, and give all the glory to God, whose face will shine brightly with sincerity despite perilous times in the past. In fact, he welcomes contact with danger because his mind is sharpened and quickened as he acts with virtue of heart and integrity of conduct, tending to instruction.

The double *khân* hexagram indicates perilous circumstances, being caught in a cavity yet in possession of sincerity needed to emerge successfully. He governs the sciences and all the arts, leads us to obtain victory by protecting our city, and within the protected walls of the city he reveals the secrets of nature by inspiring philosophers and sages. He learned about perversity and charlatanism, so now as a restored and distinguished servant, he invokes the name of the Lord in recompense and sincerity.

Phenex has endured through conditions that were sordid and degrading, dirty and perilous. His journey seemed to take one unfortunate turn after another into traps and various dead ends, one narrow passage after another, with humble opportunities to celebrate life with simple earthenware. His master sees that he learned important lessons and has much to offer. But his first life ended unceremoniously without having learned or finished the course; he was tied and bound with strong cords, then thrown into a thicket of thorns by an evil adversary under the moonlight. His redemption came in the next life through the resurrection.

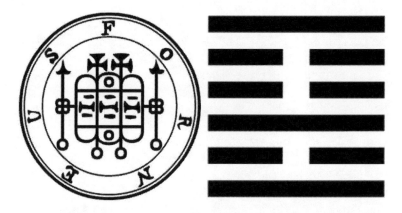

[3] *Forneus* governs the animal kingdom and watches over the generation and maintenance of beings, through medical science, chemistry, surgery, and anatomy, all of which he performs with extreme patience and positive hope. One of his specialties is the art of rhetoric and speaking in tongues, which he teaches to man. He developed this talent anciently when he took the form of a giant sea monster with symmetrical and cooperative hemispheres of sensory organs, mirror images of each other. He became his own witness, became self-aware, and found that he could verify the truth with his own wisdom and testimony. His twenty-nine legions are partially of the order of Thrones and partially Angels.

Forneus is the fallen incarnation of *Aornael*, who also has a special relationship with Lelahael in the grand scheme of things, because they seek unity with the Almighty God and have found hope and trust in the Lord from their inception. As David wrote in *Psalms 71:5*, he waits patiently upon the Lord and appoints other creatures and formations. He provides consolation to those in sorrow and despair, helping them to adopt similar patience.

A distinctive feature of Forneus is his magnificent adornment (*pî*) or ornamentation, which is not only a skill but also a habit that he has developed for all eternity. He is "brilliance arrested", or "elegance and intelligence regulated", and he can make use of very little to create inspired beauty. He is not the greatest leader, but he proves his worth and value in secondary ways. He walks on his own, but he is also adorned (and adored) by others around, who support and uplift him.

Forneus has been instrumental in the institutional and formal ceremonials of mankind since the inception, including temple arrangements and performances. These ordinances include dramatizations, symbolism, and other sensational devices to help humans remember their divine heritage, their mission, and so on. These reminders come in degrees, with allegory and ornaments, to encapsulate eternal truths, responsibilities, and duties.

And in doing so, he throws a brilliancy around the truth to make it stand out more obviously, even to the untrained mind of man. The purpose is not one of express decisiveness or execution, but it may inspire and help us to understand the various changes in life and transformations under heaven, such as life after death, thereby regulating and beautifying the lessons, intercourses, and processes of life. The garments, tokens, signs, and dramatics of ancient temple ritualism are simple and brilliant, with initiatory cleansings, endowments, sealing ordinances, and so on, to tune our minds into the divine so that we can gain a personal witness through experience, develop a relationship with the eternal ones, practice the will of the highest intelligences, and proceed toward greater enlightenment as individuals.

With *dharana*, true concentration, we can communicate with the Seraphim of this order – the "burning ones" described in *Isaiah 6* – and share in their vehement strength.

Chapter 6 – Beauty

Foreword

From his sky throne Hlidskialf, Odin rules over all the realms with one eye, as the other lies on the ocean floor in Mimir's well. He is well informed through faithful servants, primarily his own Thoughts and Memory (symbolized by ravens Hugin and Munin), of whom Memory was his most cherished.

He has many other servants as well, such as his two wolfhounds, his eight-legged steed, and the Runes. He was the preeminent author of words upon the breath, shining with perfect splendor in a creative frenzy we can only partially comprehend while quickened by their very spirit, which chills the bones as ice, forges precious stones and metals, and bears fruit as symbolized by the self-replicating ring Draupnir upon his finger.

The ring, along with his infallible and glittering spear, Gungnir, were created by his own formations, under his express direction. The spear point has authority, through runes engraved thereon, to establish a permanent covenant which is impossible to break. And it is said that Odin used the same spear to divide the worlds, creating the river whose waters never freeze, whose deep and murky waves separate the gods from the giants, etc.

Odin was the first to exercise yama (control) and self-sacrifice, whereby he harnessed the power of the Runes through language, and in the end, he outwits the swarthy giant Surtr of Muspelheim in the final battle, which marks the beginning of the next aeon in the eternal round of time, the next era stacked upon the former.

He is ceaseless in his activity and firm in executing his word, which is the law upon which all other blessings and curses rest. His sacrifice is sufficient and acceptable to himself, so he is the beginning and the end, the Alpha and Omega, who penetrates the abyss boldly, yet he is still subject to observation by others, and he must respect the proper timing and measurements as defined and declared in the beginning and end. His change in transformation filters down and affects all which lies below.

And despite his supernal magnificence, Odin also enjoys the company of mere mortal men who give it their best effort in life. He rewards the chosen slain warriors at Valhalla with abundant quantities of mead or hydromel, provided by his precious goats, who "continually browse on the tender leaves and twigs" on the topmost branch of Yggdrasil, the mysterious eternal tree of life.

Yet Odin himself is only a representation of the intelligence which we encounter in this upcoming chapter, whose fallen physical form is known as Bael.

The lands of Aychael grew strong

and was well supported by a network of cooperative city states.

Amdusias felt very secure now in his travels around the territory in carriages drawn by Mabahayahan horses, the mighty steeds under command of their leader Orobas. He enjoyed constant companionship of Malthus-Agla of Haymaiah, whose spiritual advice was always timely. And he felt blessed by his recent acquaintances in the northern territories, such as with Phenex, whom he called at times to discuss details of far-away lands.

The new seaport city of Samigina was thriving under the lead of the mighty Herahaelian Orias, and the land was well-protected through a successful trading network and a defensive agreement with Bune of Haaiah. But a nefarious combination of men had developed in the land, operating in the shadows as a scourge and an ongoing curse for the establishment, selling sorceries and numbing the once-noble minds of the inhabitants, giving place for wild spirits to possess their bodies.

This rise of a wicked combination was due to dishonesty, secrecy, desperation, and the desire for wealth.

Orias suspected corruption at the highest levels of government, and he questioned Bune, who pretended to know nothing of it. But Orias observed and decided to leverage this evil to maintain order and control in the cities. He found that the criminals and suspicious characters were easy to control and would serve as informants and spies in their desperate situation, because they were possessed or haunted by demons.

These possessed individuals would easily believe the deceit and lies of others, because they had no ability to discern the truth within themselves, so they were quick to follow whichever rumors and lies prevailed in the lands, giving into conspiracies and always suspecting their secret brethren the most.

Orias used the police and courts to round up all these criminals and force them into his service through coercion, with offers of leniency to those who complied and completed assigned tasks. Thus, Orias maintained a stronghold of control over Samigina and the surrounding cities roundabout.

Meanwhile, Andras, Andrealphus, and Glasya-Labolas returned from the northern lands, both glad and confused to find that their treasury had been restocked in Mahashiah. They were concerned that their security had been breached so easily and discretely, and they felt outsmarted by an intelligent criminal mastermind who now controlled them by administering gifts anonymously and spreading cheer around the city.

Despite protests from Glasya-Labolas, who believed that this was a trick perpetrated by Forneus or Amdusias to control them, Andras prayed for guidance on the matter. He presented his question to the Lord for guidance and awaited the answer.

But no answer came, and he became preoccupied by the ever-expanding business of governing the land.

Time passed.

Days passed, then weeks and months into winter chill and rains, and they went on about their business.

They enjoyed a bountiful harvest all year long and remained industrious through the winter solstice. The major festival of the winter season was especially cheerful this year as a rare blanket of snow fell and covered their streets and housetops.

Music filled the air with cheerful melodies and choruses, as carolers sang praise to herald the return of their Savior and King, and the northward progression of the Sun. Children danced, while elders pondered the great mysteries and gave thanks.

But amid all the celebration, Andras was unsettled in his soul, and he felt unsure how to proceed. He felt an urge to return to the north to learn more about the temple, but he wasn't sure.

So, on a Spring day, he held up his hands in a desperate petition to the Lord, and he asked the Lord to guide him.

"If you strengthen the grip in my right hand, I will go, but if you strengthen the left, I will stay."

And he squeezed his fingers with equal gentle force on each side, but he felt a stronger pulse on his right, so the answer was clear.

The Lord did not appear to him in a visible form, nor speak with a thunderous voice, but rather with a sense of light, strength, and perfection in his right hand.

So, Andras discovered his own personal Urim and Thummim, within his own soul, to be used anytime and anyplace he found himself in search of an answer.

Therefore, he received the sustaining confirmation from the Lord to return to the northern mountains for further instruction.

He trusted in the answer and proposed the idea to Andrealphus and Glasya-Labolas, who readily agreed to accompany him on the journey. And they delegated their respective responsibilities to deputies and ministers in Mahashiah before departing.

After traveling for many days, the party arrived at the point of the mountain, where they expected to see the path that they had taken with Forneus.

But the pathway was nowhere to be found, and they were confused by all the unfamiliar surroundings. The heat was becoming intense in the air, and Andras wiped sweat from his brow after arising from supplication to his God.

"This terrain looks different," exclaimed Glasya-Labolas.

And while pondering over these strange circumstances, they felt a silent warm breeze in the air, which caused them to look up and around with some alarm. The air had been completely still beforehand for days on end, so the wind was somehow unusual and aroused their curiosity.

Andras had a unique sense of his surroundings, partially due to his sharpened sense of smell, which enabled him to detect even the smallest creatures in the vicinity by their scent, along with a keen sense of orientation and movement all around.

He could sense something moving in the nearby bushes, so he surveyed the terrain quickly with his ultra-fast eye movements, zooming in and out, moving left and right with blinding speed until he located the source of the movement.

Glasya-Labolas also detected a movement and stood up straight, issuing a silent order to his first officer with a nod of his head, his wings poised in a ready position.

Andrealphus scanned the area and the skies above, flustered by some unknown anomaly in his routine mental gyrations.

A pack of fast-moving amphibians scuttled across the ground, and Andras noticed a massive cloud mounting high up in the air, up ahead on the mountaintop.

"What is that?" uttered Glasya-Labolas with a hushed tone, pointing to the valley below, which mysteriously filled with a thick frothy mist, obscuring the land and adding to the stress.

The midday skies seemed to darken, yet the Sun was still brilliant and flashed with an unusual flame in the darkness.

Andras felt a surge of fear travel down his spine, and he knew they were in the presence of a mighty being. Should he fall to his knees in reverent worship? Ascend the mountaintop?

But Andras stood firm, and he spoke softly to Glasya-Labolas and Andrealphus. "Assign your legions to hold this position, and we three will ascend the mountain to learn more about the source of this energy."

The others agreed with a nod. Their senses were severely impaired by the misty veil surrounding them, but they took courage as a group to ascend together.

Andras could perceive his surroundings best within the mist, so he took the lead while the others followed.

On ascending the mountain, they witnessed the large plume of smoke in the air as it precipitated into the mist, then condensed and crystallized in front of them, taking on various geometric forms in the air.

They looked at each other in wonder, as if they couldn't believe what they were seeing, nodding to affirm that this was not just a figment of their imaginations.

The entity moved in very close, then re-crystallized again in the general form of a man to match the appearance of these travelers, yet still sparkling with brilliant colors in a glowing haze of light. It extended its hands and touched each of them, squeezing their hands in turn, as if to reassure them that it was a tangible being and not merely an apparition.

Then it backed away, surrounded by more than sixty other lights swarming around in various beautiful shapes behind the leader, sometimes becoming translucent or completely invisible.

Andras, Andrealphus, and Glasya-Labolas were completely dumbfounded, at a loss of words, awaiting whatever came next.

Finally, Andras found the nerve to speak.

"Mighty one, we come in peace. What may we call you, and what is your purpose? How may we help you?"

The strange being responded with a hoarse voice that resonated like an old church bell, deep into their souls like a beautiful song, piercing like the perfect and glittering spear of destiny.

"I am Bael, who serves the Mighty Vehuviah."

The voice seemed to emanate from a chorus of the entire legion, which rotated around the central figure in a morphing mandala of mirrored geometric shapes, changing colors and intensity in a beautiful synchronized fiery arrangement.

The entity spoke and moved with patience. And it spoke with a still small voice, very familiar and reassuring to each of them, with metaphors and various forms of light and intelligence.

Andras, Andrealphus, and Glasya-Labolas watched and listened with intent, totally astonished, and humbled by the experience. They glowed with a special glow, somehow quickened by the Spirit to endure the flashes of celestial flame that encircled them. Andrealphus finally fell the ground, but the other two stood their ground and waited to learn what Bael had in store for them.

Why would Bael[1] descend from his sky throne to visit them?

Bael came with five major commands, which he emblazoned upon a loose slab of rock with his fiery forefinger.

Each command was represented by a single word upon the rock, which translate roughly to:

First, *non-violence*.

Second, *truthfulness*.

Third, *non-stealing*.

Fourth, *continence* or *celibacy*.

Fifth, *non-greed*.

Bael conveyed his entire history in a flash of intelligent light, and the three learned that Bael was the first among the fallen, and the ruler of the East. And he learned the path of repentance.

He felt committed to Vehuviah, the Great Self-Existent One.

Bael paused with veneration as he spoke the name of Vehuviah, and he looked up with praise as he spoke, "the source of all my glory and the strength to lift my head."

"These five commands are the basic conditions of repentance, and the source of all self-control," he explained in simple terms. Then he paused to recollect, and he recalled the distant past.

"After my fall, I learned to cry out in repentance and worship, and I learned to use these five principles to originate the forms. I used my spear to carve out the great divide between the worlds, giving passage for the deep and murky waves of the great sea to separate the dwellings."

Andras was not sure if he was referring to the Great Waters in the west, or something far greater, as in the divide that separates the celestial orbs in the heavens.

Bael's words shone with perfect splendor in a creative fiery frenzy which could chill the bones as ice, forge the precious stones and metals, and bear fruit through the mysterious process of his own self-replicating formations.

Then Bael reassembled into the form of a magnificent bird with only one eye, and he traveled upwards upon the wind.

Andras watched with wonder as two ravens followed after Bael.

Then Bael made one final pronouncement from high in the air, with a subdued tone. "The day feels heavy, and I crave counsel, but Vehuviah is quiet and only observes at the present moment, awaiting our decisions and self will."

He looked around to observe the surroundings, and he looked inward upon himself with careful reflection and consideration. Then he looked up, and a shade of deep red emerged in his complexion and surroundings, to match the setting Sun.

"I would rather keep working, but I need to slow down and rest. I despise the withdrawal of the Spirit which follows slumber; it feels so empty! But we must rest and start again in the morning, with prayer and repentance. Tomorrow, I develop a new form. My initial attempt was unsuccessful, but I will start over again with a slight change, a little slower at first."

Andras and Glasya-Labolas listened intently, realizing that he was not only narrating his own plans, but also showing them the pattern that they should follow. They were deeply impressed by the determination and ceaseless ambition of this powerful Bael, who would never rest on his laurels.

Then Bael flew off, and the clouds dissipated around him to reveal the deep-red setting sun in the west.

"What happened?" squawked Andrealphus, having awakened. "Apparently the storm has passed, thank God! Did I pass out?"

"Silence," hushed Glasya-Labolas, sitting next to the campfire, studying the runes that were etched into the stone tablet.

The night had passed, and the bright morning star Venus was visible in the East, preceding the sunrise.

Andras marveled at its beauty and brightness.

"Let us travel to the eastern mountain range, for I believe something awaits us there."

Andrealphus contemplated briefly while surveying Venus and the surrounding celestial bodies, then responded energetically. "I agree! This is a fine idea that will lead to excellent results." He didn't often take a strong stance like this, but when he did, Andras and Glasya-Labolas listened carefully and appreciated his perspective.

They traveled for another two days, then came upon a new valley in the east, with a thriving civilization sprawling across the land.

"The wonders of this creation never cease to amaze me," expressed Andras.

"Indeed," his companions responded together, both nodding as they looked out upon this advanced society and wondered what awaited them.

As they traveled into the heart of the city, they witnessed many things that seemed quite familiar at first, like street vendors, brick and mortar buildings, parks and recreational activities, citizens bustling from location to location, some on foot and others in carts, kids playing games in the alleys, riding bicycles, and so on, and so on.

But other things were strange and unfamiliar, like carts that moved without any animals to pull them, brilliant streetlamps, colorful animated signs, various tubes and suspended cables running along the roadways, magnificent multi-tiered bridges over the city's main river, and other miracles of technology.

They walked into the heart of the city uncontested, never questioned by any police nor curious citizens.

They wandered inconspicuously because the citizens were busy preparing for some sort of celebration, with hordes of people bustling around, many dressed in fancy costumes and masks, others playing in musical bands, some selling food and wares, and others gathering supplies and setting up for what would become a massive celebration all day and night.

A large parade with well over two hundred carts moved along the central road, met with cheers every step of the way.

Citizens of the town yelled with great excitement to greet and honor the passing procession, with praise and veneration.

"Long live the Order of Dominions! Praise Paimon our King!"

At the head of the parade was a gargantuan dragon with purple and yellow scales, appearing real at first, but in fact it was only a representation upheld by men under a massive canopy. Its large head and arms moved independently and danced to the music, while its tail slithered and waved in large circular motions.

After the procession passed, they heard a bard singing joyfully in the street, playing his guitar to a group of happy listeners:

"Praised be our Lord Paimon[2], who has ascended the throne!
Oh, give thanks to Lord Paimon, for he was born in weakness,
But gained power and strength as he conquered with fear,
Then gained the spirit of Haziael and learned to show mercy.
He has built friendships and favor for us all,
For he is good, and his steadfast love endures!

"Such pomp and circumstance! Whatever are they celebrating?" wondered Andras aloud to his companions while marveling over the fanfare. "If only we enjoyed such unity in Mahashiah...."

The city was called Goro Paimona, named after King Paimon, and the civilization was known as Haziael.

Who and where was this Great Paimon?

Andras, Andrealphus, and Glasya-Labolas asked about Paimon, but they were only told in obscure terms that he was currently "lying in the deep". They learned that the procession was symbolic of the angels and potentates, those loyal to Paimon. The two most important angels were known as Labal and Abali, his principal consorts, but it was unclear whether any were physically in attendance at this celebration.

"They are watching from below, and they are pleased with us," said one of the merry townsfolk. "They are here in spirit!"

The three travelers enjoyed a meal and some drinks in a local popular tavern, where they discussed more on this fascinating culture and their god-king. They wondered when they might be able to make the acquaintance of Paimon or his inner circle.

One patron at the bar was apparently drunk beyond his limits, cussing and yelling in a huff, then lamenting all his woes aloud.

He made such a ruckus that the bartender finally had to request security and have him thrown out to the street, where he tumbled in the dirt.

Andras was curious and wondered if this man might lead them to something more interesting, or share some helpful information, due to his drunken and forthcoming state of mind. So, he told the others to wait while he followed up with this man.

The man was glad to have a companion, and he continued blathering along without any reservations. He had a beautiful rich voice and put on the pretense of confidence as he talked, but it was evident his pride was deeply wounded somehow after an unfortunate series of events in his life.

"I am a wicked, vile, and worthless soul, you see... and the best sort at that! When my Lord fell, I was the first to fall with him, when we were the worthier sort, not like these mindless idiots!"

As the man continued talking, Andras felt dizzy and disoriented, and the sound faded low, so he could see the man talking but he couldn't hear any words.

He looked around as his peripheral vision faded into darkness, then looked again at the man and saw a vision of him sitting within a chariot of fire, flanked by two beautiful angels.

Was he imaging this, or was it real?

He snapped back into reality. The audio returned, and his vision became clear in an instant.

Then the man continued, "If only Bael would endorse my offer!"

"Excuse me. Bael?" interrupted Andras, intrigued that the man knew of Bael.

"Yes of course. He has ignored my call for help. I've distributed presentations and senatorships, favors and all good familiars...," he spoke confusingly. "What else could Bael require of me?

And yet he pits me against Paimon! I should have known this was all a great trick at my expense!"

"And what is your name, stranger?" asked Andras.

"Belial, Belial, once of... never mind! I have a new quest now, but it's a... dreadful one." His speech was slurring to a halt.

"Belial[3], my name is Andras. My companions are in the tavern. May we accompany you back to your homestead? We may be able to help each other."

But Belial passed out and tumbled to the dirt once again.

Andras left him on the ground and headed back inside the tavern to follow up with Andrealphus and Glasya-Labolas.

"He speaks like a drunken sarcastic idiot," explained Andras, "but also speaks of his business all around the wider kingdom."

Andras thought of sharing his vivid vision of the fiery chariot, but he stopped himself and continued. "He knows about Bael. Perhaps he may provide clues after he sobers up."

The others agreed, and Glasya-Labolas hoisted the drunken Belial over his broad shoulders, and they went along their way. They wanted to take shelter for the evening at the inn, but they could not find any room due to the massive celebration, which brought visitors in from the surrounding lands. The party was still raging late into the night, fireworks flashing in the skies, music playing, and joyous people all around. They decided to exit the city limits once again and rejoin their traveling party.

And the night passed, and the morning arrived.

Belial was the last to wake. He was startled by his surroundings, but then he remembered Andras and remained calm despite the binds on his wrists.

"My people will pay handsomely for my safe return," he started. "Who are you, and what do you want?"

Andras was the first to respond. "Belial, we have no intention to harm you or demand any ransom. You were a danger to yourself and others last night, so we brought you to neutral ground..."

"Neutral ground?" retorted Belial, looking around at the strangers and holding up his bound hands.

"It was just a precaution. We will loosen the binds. We would like to discuss on peaceful terms, but if you prefer, we will let you go freely and be on our way. We would like to set up business dealings with this city of Goro...."

"Hah! The city of Goro Paimona. You must have me all wrong. I am not from this city, but merely passing through on business."

"Perhaps we can discuss further, and something may work...," Andras started, but he stopped when he sensed danger nearby.

Glasya-Labolas also detected something, and he was wide-eyed as he whisked his head around, scanning for an imminent threat.

"You may have noticed that you are surrounded," said Belial with a crooked smile on his face, eyes glowing deep fiery red.

The area was surrounded now with a horde of unknown creatures in hoods, moving in slowly.

"It took you long enough!" howled Belial.

One of the hooded men responded, "Our sincerest apologies."

"I suppose I should be grateful the beacon device still works. Thank you. Now listen, you, Andras. Now we're on more agreeable neutral grounds. You're outnumbered, so untie me now or there will be serious consequences...."

Andras held up his hands in peace and moved toward Belial to untie the cord around his wrists.

"Listen Belial, I meant what I said before. Let us negotiate. Your business dealings in Goro Paimona were unsuccessful, but we come from the west. Maybe we can help each other."

Andras and Andrealphus were interested to make peace, but Glasya-Labolas was not so convinced and growled disapproval.

Andras was not intimidated by a fight either, but he preferred to practice his skills with verbal communication and negotiation.

Belial was impressed by their persistence and decided to listen. His eyes changed color once again, this time to a yellowish hue, less intimidating but still intense and serious.

"Stand down," he said to his legions.

So, the four leaders sat together in the main tent and discussed, while the other groups mingled outside, a bit tensely at first. Some of the henchmen erupted into some harsh words and a minor skirmish, but others stepped in and quelled the episode.

The mood finally lightened as meal preparations began, and sweet-smelling meat, herbs, and spices filled the air.

Andras was very interested to find out that Belial, besides being a cutthroat businessman and skilled negotiator in political affairs, was also an avid curator of countryside and gardens.

Belial's mood brightened as he began talking about his hobby, and his hope to preserve the health of his people with herbs, plants, and other agriculture. "I take great pride in developing the lands and providing for our people," he said.

But his happy countenance was replaced by a morose look, and he hesitated before continuing.

"The truth is that I have a lot of ground to make up, to pay for my past sins. I've conjured plagues – famines, harmful insects, even sterility – against my enemies in the past.

"And I brought similar plagues upon my own people as a result. I thought my anger and passion would pay off, but it took on a life of its own and led to my terrible demise, in dim days of the past which I'd rather forget."

Andras, Andrealphus, and Glasya-Labolas were impressed by his honesty and felt somehow assured that his intentions were noble.

"So, I have a duty to fulfill, and my work is beginning to pay off. Some of my previous enemies are less forgiving and fall into the same trap of hatred I know well, but others accept my offerings. Last year was not very great, but the growth comes in cycles. But this year we've had an overabundance of offspring and fruits, and the lands are fecund and fertile as never before. Part of our success is due to a new system we've developed for metering and distributing the runoff from the lake."

The others were listening intently.

"We don't have all the advanced technology of the Haziaelians," he continued, speaking about the inhabitants of Goro Paimona and its surroundings, "but we have a special spirit of industry and happiness among our people now."

What interested Andras the most was listening to him talk about his people with such devotion.

"Besides," Belial admitted with a return to his former sarcasm, "we're not a mere hive which worships the great evil dragon! But... I digress. Perhaps we can eventually find some degree of peace and trade with them. Right now, they are just too selfish, hiding under covers, living in their own exclusive... heaven.

"Of course," he continued, "we understand the importance of drawing up sensible boundaries to protect the sanctity of our assigned stewardships. Some relationships are not meant to be... for now. But in the meantime, we are simply doing what we can to nurture peaceful progression of our people, to acknowledge the Great Spirit in all things great and small."

"Why the hostility in Paimona?" asked Glasya-Labolas frankly.

"Well," he sighed. I still have my weaknesses, friend. I live in the flesh among men and beasts who praise and pride themselves rather than God, as they ought. And, well... I fell into same trap, reacting with anger, making myself guilty of the same crime."

He paused to contemplate while the others still listened, anticipating that he still had more on his mind.

"The mighty Bael challenged me to leave behind my old ways and remember who I really am. I feel you are the latest blessing from the Lord, who gives bountifully to those who will humble themselves and seek, respect His Word, and enact righteousness in life... and death!"

Belial trailed off in thought.

Andrealphus chimed in for the first time. "You are mighty with your testimony, Belial, because you have gained experience and you know right from wrong. You have done much to stir souls of the living and the dead in the spirit, awakening them to their respective callings. So, I thank you. We can help each other."

They traveled another two days to the south and entered a small town on the border of Belial's lands. Thousands of goats roamed around the mountainside, browsing leaves and twigs of the trees, as a shepherd dog came running up to greet them.

"Ahoy, Lerad! Good boy!" exclaimed Belial to the happy dog. "Run and tell your master I've returned with some new friends."

The dog was overjoyed with excitement and scurried toward the farmhouse in a flash.

"I trust you'll join me for a drink at the hut," he said, pointing to a building beside the farmhouse. "Thanks to the precious goats, we have the finest mead and hydromel in the world."

Over drinks, they shared stories and made confessions to clear their minds. Not all was well in this land, nor back in Mahashiah, so they had many problems to discuss, and solutions to share.

One of their concerns had to do with managing the criminals.

"We throw the offenders into jail cells, but we hope they see the light and decide to change. Some never see it and waste away, but we're ready to assist all who help themselves," explained Belial as Glasya-Labolas nodded knowingly.

"Of course, we're all interconnected, so we find that what's best for them is also best for all of us.

"Sometimes it's painful to watch them sit and wallow in misery, but we do our best to serve and provide for the most depraved. And it pays off in the end, as many of them turn into some of the most productive citizens when they finally see that we're all in this together, working toward a common goal for our society."

"What a fine civilization you have here, Belial," said Andras, looking up at the brilliant sun, enjoying the terrain and company.

[1] *Bael* can destroy a man or empower him to the loftiest heights.

The purpose of this research and this story is to invoke the latter, not only for the benefit of the reader, but also for the good of Bael himself, whose eternal destiny and identity is none other than the one known as *Vehuviah* or Jehovah, who is raised and exalted above all things. Bael is the third and most beautiful of the Briatic creations, and the originator of the Forms (Yetsirah), and the seat or foundation of harmony, mildness, and peace.

His is the still small voice which speaks to mankind with the highest and holiest form of communion, the spirit of revelation and prophecy, which leads us to cry in repentance and worship. He travels on the wind like a magnificent bird, which hears all calls and speaks with a beautiful song to the soul of men, piercing like the infallible and glittering spear of destiny.

Bael would have been lost forever if it were not for Vehuviah, who dwells primarily in the region of fire. He is marked and known by his uncanny ability to withstand and harness the flashes of celestial flame issued by the great swarthy demon.

He is the first and the last to transmute that dark ominous cloud into bright energy, which is made possible by (and resulting in the furtherance of) his subtlety and great wisdom, which breeds an unmatched enthusiasm for science and the arts.

He can undertake the most difficult things, accomplishing them in due time and order. It is with such worshipful veneration and adoration that the ancients recognized him by his corresponding divine name, יהוה.

This acknowledgement will arouse in the astute reader a sense of the absolute and reverent worship, devoted and sincere, which is due to Vehuviah the Lord, as I may address him.

Some readers may have a difficult time accepting that he could have a fallen nature at all, considering his apparent infallibility and perfection, for he personifies the great Urim and Thummim, or the Lights and Perfection of heaven.

But perhaps it is due to his eternal goodness and perfection that he assumes responsibility for fallen Bael. He unites with the fallen spirit as a single entity, taking sins upon himself by proxy, redeeming Bael and all of us to allow eternal coexistence and to complete his plan of salvation.

Bael can be thought of as the assistant of Vehuviah and the first principal spirit, who rules in the east with his sixty-six legions of infernal spirits. He can transform himself into diverse shapes, and he can also take on multiple forms simultaneously and cause others to be invisible. His mannerisms are well calculated and full of patience, which reflects in his wise hoarse voice.

And yet, he still cries out for protection from his grand creator, whom he acknowledges as the source of all his glory and the strength to lift his head. He ultimately understands that there are conditions of repentance which center around the idea of *yama*, control and abstinence, as captured in the famous mantra,

"Ahimsa satya asteya brahmacharya aparigraha"

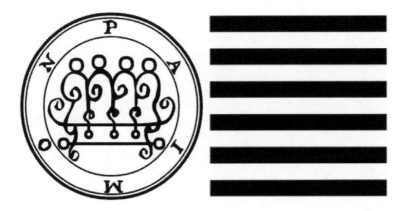

[2] *Paimon* is the great king, obedient to Lucifer, with 200 legions of spirits at his command, among them angels and potentates.

His order has been known as the Order of Dominions, which – when acting with ideal unity – is capable of almost all miracles and works known to man, including those of the earth, the mind, the waters, the sciences and arts, and the musical instruments.

The order of Paimon's creation and identity is inverted from the traditional (mis-)conception that all things are created spiritually first before physical creation. Paimon was created by Bael in a *fallen* physical state with extraordinary power and all potential, yet he was subject to hatred, suffering from hypocrisy and pride.

Eventually he comes to fulfill his destiny and eliminate these negative traits, but he was bones and flesh before spiritual birth, so to speak. (And yet in the eternal scheme of things, the order doesn't matter, since the end is the beginning.)

So, we say that Paimon *learned* to forgive and extend mercy, and he teaches the same to others.

He almost always travels in a procession with great pomp and fanfare and celebration, which may obfuscate the raw power and wisdom of which he is capable.

In the beginning, he was wise enough to ally himself with others who were likeminded, firm and correct like himself, to create a stronger and more powerful whole. He fulfills all his promises, and he expects the same from others, always renewing covenants with the highest expectations and seeing the best and brightest in others, even more than they see in themselves at first.

He is known in the eternities as הזיאל (Haziael) the merciful, who grants friendship and the favor it facilitates.

He allows reconciliation based on a New Hope; a new promise, made sincerely with trust and good faith. He found in so doing, we become more powerful and beneficent – more creative and constructive – than ever before, in all eternity.

So now he feels good, and he recognizes extraordinary potential and new light ahead.

Consider the parable: he begins as a proud dragon lying hidden in the deepest cavern in all the heavens. He emerges with some help and motivation from an external source, and he becomes curious about what lies ahead and beyond, so he enters the field and learns how to play with activity and vigilance all day long.

But at night, he returns to the depths in a slumber, exhausted, and he awakes in a sluggish mood in the morning. The cycle continues for a time; despite his sluggishness he feels motivated to move by the mystery of the vast open space all around him.

The young dragon seems to be leaping up but is still in the depths of ignorance. But over time he learns to extend and use his wings to fly, awkwardly at first, and eventually he gains more skill and precision. There's so much to see and experience!

Sometimes he falls or overextends himself, and he sees a pattern: he is likely to fail when he isn't paying attention or when he is distracted by such feelings as hatred or spite. So, he learns to be more peaceful and graceful, and he thrives on the energy of playing friendly and compassionately with others.

He enjoys the physical experience, feeling powerful and solid, yet he also experiences hunger and realizes there is something even more powerful in the emptiness, until finally he sings out in praise like David in the 106th Psalm:

"Praise the LORD! Oh, give thanks to the LORD, for he is good, and his steadfast love endures forever."

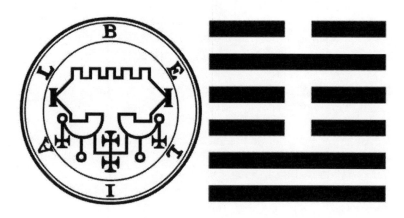

[3] Also very close to Lucifer is the fallen spirit and powerful king known as *Belial*, appearing with his "two beautiful angels sitting in a chariot of fire".

He's made a name for himself, albeit wicked and vile, yet he is proud of that name and his backstory, which he enjoys retelling. He has a beautiful voice, and he declares with some false pride (although sore inside) that he was created next after Lucifer and that he "fell first from among the worthier sort".

He takes his fall seriously and his duties in stride, managing his fifty legions and answering truly to those who either serve him or constrain him with divine power. But outside the business of distributing presentations and senatorships, giving favors and good familiars, he is quite dishonest and cynical in his approach.

His eternal nature is not so wicked, vile, or worthless, and he is known as חבויה (Xabuviah), who gives liberally and celebrates the past, present, and future of the Lord's ministry upon the earth.

He recounts abundant blessings which the Lord has poured forth upon those who seek and respect his word, humble themselves, and enact righteousness in their lives. He discourages disputes and contention among men, and instead promotes the peaceful unity and happy progress of the Saints, for the preservation of health and the healing of the sick.

He helps us to understand that not all relationships are meant to be saved. Drawing up boundaries and protecting the sanctity and integrity of one's assigned stewardship is vitally important in the eternal plan of the Lord. He cautions us to set aside distractions and vanity of the flesh, which desires to praise itself, and instead to acknowledge the Lord's spirit in all things.

He preserves health and heals the sick, often through the means of herbs, plants, and other agriculture in the diverse countryside, gardens, and hunting grounds across the land. He takes a leading role in developing the lands, ensuring their fertility and growth. He feels a duty to make up for the sterility, famine, plague, and harmful insects he conjured in his dim past, and he atones for it by working to harvest an abundance of offspring and fruits, enough reward for him to continue with his efforts in eternity.

This sort of growth comes in spurts, with intervals of regrouping (as a bamboo grows with joints). He progresses steadily with attention paid to "proper regulations", which he accepts and enacts with style and grace sweetly. Water overflows the lake, which is carefully measured and controlled to make regular divisions in the flow, to pool resources, and create regularity.

So, in the end, Belial teaches us what he has learned, which is faith, repentance, and confession, encouraging others to imagine the best of each other, resolve difficulties and estrangement, and create friendships with a relaxed and rational approach and gifts.

Chapter 7 – Victory

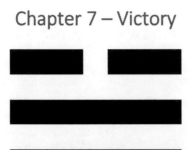

Foreword

So now we move to the first of the "forms", the Yetsiratic portion of the universe, יצר, which implies not only the form and fashion, but also being bound, confined, and straitened like the biological entity formed in the womb, consisting of genetic material and the makings of a body, which is fundamental in the eternal plan of salvation provided by God for man and all sentient life forms.

It manifests as the physical body, into which God breathes (נפח) the breath (נשמה or רוח) of life or soul life (נשמת חיים) to seal a soul having life (נפש חיה). So, it is fundamental to the creation.

The one who best exemplifies this energy in the Norse traditions is the goddess Freyja ("Lady"), sister and counterpart of Frey, who rules love, fertility, battle, and death.

Freyja loves animals. She has two cats who draw her chariot, and Hildisvini, the bristled battle-boar whom she often rides and considers to be her friend. She also often wears a cloak of falcon feathers, which is imbued with magical properties that allow her to fly and change into the form of a falcon.

She also loves men and women, and she takes pleasure in entertaining half of the heroes slain in battle in her Great Hall.

Her beauty is beyond description and often attracts the attention of various men, giants, and dwarves, such as the four dwarves who tricked her into spending time with them in exchange for a brilliant gleaming necklace, Brisingamen. This enchanted item became a focal point of sad stories and scandalous accusations, and she hasn't outlived her ill repute, whether deserved or not. Many jealous observers accused her of greed and lasciviousness, and they still shame her for having taught the secrets of Vanir witchcraft to the Aesir.

But the one she loves the most is her husband Odr, whose frequent absence causes her great pain and grief. Lady Vanadis, as she is known, is the mother of our rituals and observances, starting with the division of time into periods, the day and night, the heavenly firmament separating internal waters from external, the assignment of the lights and earthly creations into divisions, plants and animals reproducing, and finally the creation of man and woman, with love between them, productivity and fertility, splendid and joyous with flaxen energy of the earth and fruition.

She travels throughout the world, still seeking her husband and weeping tears of gold.

The earth cries out with Freyja, as she cries for her lost Odr. "When will he be found again?"

Among the blessings made possible by her mourning, her effort, and her tears of searching and awaiting, is the strong, rich, and salty soil, which allows the transformation from decaying matter into awesome forms of life.

And now we meet Agares, who like Freyja has been depressed for a time, feeling heavy and humid, and exhausted as he confronts and endures these feelings and observances.

Belial was quite fond of his visitors

and took great pride in showing them the mountains and the countryside, in the lush land named Xabuviah after his ancestry. He invited them to stay for a while, and they eagerly accepted.

"We came here on an omen with promise for future success," explained Andras. "Master Belial, what else can you tell us about the great Bael? Apparently, both of us have been blessed to have been visited by his great presence."

"Well!" started Belial as he drank from his hydromel concoction. "Bael, the assistant of Vehuviah! Yes, we have been blessed."

All four of them exchanged glances, and Andrealphus looked down in embarrassment, since he was the only one who failed to withstand the presence of Bael.

Andras felt himself becoming dizzy again. His periphery faded to black, and he saw Belial once again, with two angels flanking him in a chariot of fire.

Then he blinked and furrowed his brow. The vision vanished.

"Let me tell you..." continued Belial, trailing off in thought. Then he continued, "Bael is an enigma, yes, and I don't know much about him, but I know about his formations."

"What do you mean? What formations?" asked Glasya-Labolas.

"Well, Bael, commanded by his master Vehuviah, took the products of creation and mastered, above all, the art of forming and fashioning the creations into... entities. He is the supreme organizer, who can bind up all the elements, then confine and straiten them into the various bodies of all salient lifeforms."

Belial stopped to glance at the confused but interested looks from the others, then continued, "The truth is, I don't understand it all very well myself...."

"Forms animated by the breath of life," interjected Andrealphus.

"Why yes," Belial said with surprise, delighted that somebody seemed to understand him. "I know a certain man, southwest from our present location, who claims with boldness to be the *first form on the Earth*. So, if you're interested...."

"We're interested," asserted Andras. "When can we leave?"

The fellowship wasted no time. They prepared to depart on the following morning, to travel southwest and extend their journey. This journey would take them through the outskirts of the land called Yelial, where Andras, Andrealphus, and Glasya-Labolas had never traveled before.

Accompanying them was a party of twelve others, their most trusted advisors. And the others left behind were instructed to organize a messaging relay network and learn more about the technology of the Haziaelians.

The sixteen travelers would need to either cross the river that descended from the western mountains into a massive lake or circumnavigate the lake entirely. In either case the terrain would be difficult to pass and muddy at times, due to the large amount of runoff from the river this year. They would travel on foot, with just a small number of pack mules to accompany them with provisions and supplies, and the plan was to travel southwesterly until they arrived at the fork in the road, then choose whether to traverse the river or pass around the lake.

The good news was that no matter which direction they took, they would be surrounded by piney forests with plenty of game, berries, and usable firewood for their journey.

So, the next morning, they set out on the path, led by Belial and Glasya-Labolas.

"Let's go!" barked Glasya-Labolas impatiently. He was eager to get on the road and explore the forestland along the way.

They traveled for a day and reached the valley of the lake, which extended off into the southern horizon like a great sea, almost as far as the eyes could see.

The river was surging down from the northern mountains, and it fed into the lake in a large delta surrounded by mudflats.

"This seems like an easy decision," said Andrealphus.

"Yes, it does," answered Andras, looking to Belial for validation. "It seems we should circle the lake, because these waters are...." He trailed off, searching for the right word but never finding it.

"Yes indeed," confirmed Belial. "The last time I came this way, the river was less intimidating.... It will take a few days to travel around, but...."

Belial stopped and stood upright with his eyes transfixed toward the south. His usual plain appearance lit up with fiery energy, and his countenance blazed with a special determination which caused all the others to follow his gaze. Then he pointed to the south and spoke in a soft voice, "There he is."

Andras saw what looked like a human in the distance, and he squinted to get a better view of its form. And then, he looked up and noticed a large sparrowhawk flying overhead, with its short wings outstretched, circling above the group, then floating down to land on the man's fist.

It was an old man riding toward them on a massive crocodile, carrying the goshawk upon his fist.

The bird ruffled its feathers, nestling its short wings into place, then breathed deeply in through its beak as if to compose itself, while the man strode toward them.

There were other goshawks in the air as well, swirling around in formations, and they were interested and came down to inspect the scene, perching in the trees, and feasting on the ripe fruit.

Andras noticed that the fruit on the trees maturing rapidly, with low-hanging fruits occasionally falling to the ground, absorbing quickly into the rich fertile soil.

The man spoke through large lips loudly.

"Why have you returned, Belial, and with such a pathetic party?"

Belial nodded in respect, then answered, "Oh ancient one, Agares of Yelial, I have returned to learn more, and I brought these companions because they have been favored to meet Bael, who formed our mortal frames from the dust. They are young and naïve, but they are humble and desirous to learn from you. We expected to see you on the other side...."

"Silence, Belial. You think I didn't anticipate your arrival?"

Belial's spirit crumbled to the ground as Agares[1] upbraided him.

"I apologize, Master Agares. Surely you anticipated us, and it is an honor to be in your presence again." He wanted to say more, but he stopped short and nervously waited for a reply.

Agares continued, *"The young Ravenhead here would have been wise to respect his elders and follow their advice. But instead, he has traveled a long errant path. Such a waste of precious time, energy, and life. A rebel without a cause!"*

"And the Peacock," he continued, motioning his free hand toward Andrealphus, *"has precious gifts but squanders them on fruitless pursuits like a fool chasing after the wind. When will he learn to stabilize himself and his senses?"*

"And the Canine-Gryphon creature here," now motioning to Glasya-Labolas, *"wastes his strength on physical feats without using mental reasoning, and his mind is consumed with anger. He could rise to such greater nobler heights!"*

Glasya-Labolas grew furious as Agares talked, and he stepped forward with wings arched and arms outstretched to demonstrate that he was unintimidated by the strange Crocodile Man. But as he stepped toward Agares, he was shocked with a forceful surge of energy and thrown back several feet, and an invisible fortress field surrounding Agares lit up with an electric flash.

The field continued to sparkle with electricity where Glasya had made contact, as the others looked on with fear and concern.

Glasya lowered his wings and took on a more submissive stance, sufficiently chastened and ready to accept defeat.

And Agares's countenance changed as well, jarred and surprised by Glasya's attack, and suddenly grateful for the protective field. He closed his eyes and muttered something under his breath, resembling a prayer of gratitude.

Belial spoke up on behalf of the group.

"Master Belial, these men serve and fear the Lord Almighty. They have worked and made continual offerings. I know you've faced some difficulties, and you find it difficult to trust, but I ask you to give them a chance."

Agares reflected, *"The Lord again works in peculiar ways...."*

His tone was forlorn, and his eyes filled with tears as he spoke. The others were moved by his sincerity and had forgotten all about the previous exchange.

Golden raindrops began to sprinkle from the cloudy sky.

"I crave the day when she returns, when the earth is restored to its perfect crystalline glory, and she judges as the eternal provost. We will all serve in peace as she upholds justice with her sword. Her bowels are filled with mercy, compassion, and acceptance of our offerings, and now I accept your offerings as well."

Each of the others nodded in agreement, although they were somewhat confused by his ramblings.

Agares continued. "Each of us is fallible in the face of the Lord until we become perfected, and we do our best in the meantime. I apologize for my contrariness when you arrived. I am still in deep mourning, but I have recently prayed while performing my vows and due observations, searching for new hope upon which to focus my passion. Perhaps your arrival is a partial fulfillment of that hope and promise."

Andras tried to listen but became distracted as he noticed the decaying fruit, fallen from low-hanging branches, was dissolving in the rich and salty soil, transforming in the twinkling of an eye into various lifeforms, like baby sheep and small birds, as Agares continued speaking. He could hardly believe his eyes.

"As you come with the blessing and recommendation of Belial, we also trust you," finished Agares through those very large lips, which were now smiling.

Underneath him the crocodile shifted its weight and wagged its tail with some excitement. And the goshawk fluttered its wings, then flew off to join his companions in the trees, returning with fruit for each of the travelers in turn.

The fruit was delicious and edifying, imbued with special energy and vitality that Andras and the others had never felt.

"You will travel south around the lake into the Forbidden Land, at the entrance of Afrika. There you will meet a warrior riding upon a black horse near the marshy waters. Do not stay long, but learn what you can, and move to the dry plains with geese, where you will meet another. You will offer your help to these souls and learn about your own soul in the process."

The group accepted their task and offered thanks for the fruit, which would sate their appetites for days along the path.

They traveled in a southerly direction, around the massive lake, never feeling hunger for several days, until they encountered a massive marshland surrounding an estuary of another large river, which fed into the eastern sea.

"I see why this is called the Forbidden Land," said Andrealphus. "This river is larger than the other! How will we pass?"

Glasya-Labolas explained that although it is difficult and risky, he and his men could fly one person at a time over the river, but not more, as their wings were not suitable for heavy payloads.

But as he spoke, they all noticed a shadow on the ground and looked upward at a strange sight – a large deep-purple globe – floating down from the heavens with a basket underneath, descending downward slowly. Two men were peering down over the side of the basket, one of them holding an object in his left hand. Was it a weapon of some kind to bombard them?

When the large ball in the sky was within vocal range, one of the riders called down to the group.

"Who comes here?"

Belial responded confidently. "I am Belial. We come in peace, at the request of Agares of Yelial. We seek a mighty marquis."

Suddenly a rope ladder came falling to the ground, a few yards away from the group, and the voice from above spoke again.

"We expected you, and we will transport you to the palace, but we can only transport twelve."

So, Glasya-Labolas and his legionnaires offered to fly and provide security in the skies, while the others in the group boarded the flying craft.

And as they floated off into the skies, Andrealphus commented, "I couldn't have predicted this strange turn of events!"

They journeyed in the skies over the surging river and marveled at the scenery of the earth below when viewed from up above. The fertile marshlands were well developed into farmlands, vibrant with all the colors of life and the mark of civilization, and beyond the marsh was a desert with rolling dunes of sand, extending almost as far as the eye could see toward the south.

And there in the desert was a thriving civilization, an oasis of life with a large metropolis in the middle. There were pyramids and massive edifices made from artful stone blocks, citizens bustling around in marketplaces, and work crews building new structures. The most impressive structure of all was the central royal palace, flanked by two large sphinxes and surrounded with an array of guard stations, in which guards occasionally rotated positions, and a full-time army of workers carrying on about the business of the palace. Stone chimneys emitted sweet-smelling smoke, and the air was filled with floating balloons.

Each balloon was operated by a machinist who controlled a small flame to heat the air and provide lift. Andras and the others were familiar with mining and the separation of natural gases and fuels, but had never seen such a gas-powered torch, which used compressed gas and a control mechanism to adjust the strength of the flame. The machinist controlled the lateral movements with four additional levers, which controlled four small jets on the side of the craft, each of which could provide thrust and acceleration by releasing a stream of pressurized air from a canister. And a small motor hummed in the center, continually pressurizing the air in its central tank.

One structure stood out from the rest with its massive size and brilliant-white appearance.

"Kimaris rules over all parts of Afrika," explained the officer, who called himself Deanis. "He is Father of this Great House, and the reincarnation of the fourth son of Ham, who ordered the construction of the Great House and became our first God King in the Forbidden land. He is expecting you."

Andras recalled that Agares specifically instructed them to make their visit brief, then move onward to the plains. So, he listened and nodded along with the flight guide, but privately considered that they may need to plan an early escape if Kimaris[2] and the others wanted to keep them too long.

They landed gently within the courthouse of the Great House.

A delightful aroma of incense and opium filled the air, which added a smooth sheen to their sensory, as if they were entering some sort of dreamworld. People were smiling and welcoming as they ushered the visitors into an inner chamber.

Andras and Glasya-Labolas gave each other a look of suspicion, as if they both knew that something wasn't right here, but Belial led the way undeterred, and carried a conversation with Deanis as they walked the path.

The central chamber was surprisingly open to public access. Even the armed guards were laughing and indulging in the fun, sitting and lounging with the others. Many were smoking opium and herbs from their hookahs while waiters walked around with wine, meat, and fresh fruit to share with all the citizens.

Musicians played on harps, flutes, brass cymbals and other gentle percussion to fill the hall with a mesmerizing blur of exotic sounds, while some of the older men met in a formal symposium, debating philosophies in a dull passionate tone.

One man stood up to announce his point, seemingly inspired with an epiphany, but then he stumbled mid-sentence and fell to his knees, dropping a glass of wine to the ground with a shatter. The others erupted into hearty laughter while several attendants came quickly to clean up the mess and escort the old man back to his feet, still wobbling in drunkenness.

"These are the senators of our House," explained Deanis with a hushed tone, "and those who contribute money and resources to the cause. Kimaris treats them as royalty, sparing no expenses for their comfort and luxury."

He uncomfortably cleared his throat, perturbed with the scene of gluttony and excessive drinking all around him.

A woman shrieked and slapped a drunken senator as he assaulted her with wanton aggressiveness. Laughter erupted, and another man even stood up to join in assaulting her.

Belial exchanged questioning glances with the others, and he was about to intervene, but the central doors at the front of the corridor opened, and an audible cheer of drunken jubilation murmured through the hall.

Everybody stopped what they were doing and gave their full attention to the new arrival.

At the head of the hall, the principal musicians sounded off with an introductory rally, with brass horns and fully chromatic harps, to extend a special welcome as their ruler Kimaris strode slowly through the main doors on a black horse, silhouetted by a bright light in the background.

The crowd awaited in anticipation as he trotted dramatically.

Behind Kimaris came twenty more riders, ten on each side, cloaked in flaming red gowns and helmets.

"All heil Kimaris!" yelled one of the guards, and the crowd erupted with an echo of the same phrase.

"All heil Kimaris!"

Many stooped to bow in reverence, and the hall went silent.

"Lord Kimaris, we present to you for your pleasure, the sixteen men from the northern territories, just as you requested."

Andras watched Kimaris closely and felt something was wrong.

Kimaris was a mighty man, yet he was distinctly disinterested and anxious, visibly shaking in his right hand. His countenance was full of grief and despair. Then he snapped up to attention, his eyes widened, and he flipped from despondency to paranoia.

But he said nothing.

And in his presence, Andras felt empty and dark, even darker than he had already felt in this den of debauchery.

Belial felt inspired to take the lead in this awkward situation, and he spoke up with authority.

"Your honor, Lord Kimaris, we have been sent to you by Agares, who speaks highly of your valiance. We seek the southern plains. May we have your permission to travel onward in our journey?"

Kimaris dismounted his horse, then dismissed the crowd and his legion of twenty. His horse followed the others as they exited back through the main entrance.

He paused for a long moment, looking perplexed or drunken.

Then finally, he sighed deeply and spoke for the first time.

"Gentlemen, please come with me. Let us leave this place."

Belial, Andras, Andrealphus, and Glasya-Labolas followed him up through the corridor to the very end, then through another archway into an inner sanctum.

Aquatic tanks and vegetation surrounded them on all sides, teeming with life. No one spoke while they walked.

Kimaris turned to them, and they stopped in their tracks.

Despite the beautiful surroundings, they were all uncomfortable, and something nagged at them, begging to leave this place.

"I wish you came to visit during a brighter time, my friends," said Kimaris. "Conditions are such that I cannot trust even my own guards and senators. Please accept my apologies."

They introduced themselves and discussed the kingdom.

Kimaris explained that he had visited the visionary Agares, master of strange sorcery, to seek his guidance in overcoming the infestation of evil in the land. And Agares had apparently orchestrated this entire meeting in his usual mysterious manner. "Agares advised me to seek your help," he said.

"Well, it sounds like a bad situation if you can't even trust your own guards and senators!" said Belial.

Kimaris nodded and replied, "Our kingdom was based upon the celebration of life and all its simple pleasures. But now it has deteriorated into negligence and filth. These are sad days of mourning and repentance for me, my friends."

He paused, and the others listened intently.

"I have learned much from Agares," he continued. "He taught me how to be confident with gentleness and inward sincerity, and how to find *purpose* in supporting myself and all my friends. And it worked for a while, but I was careless and gathered the false light of evil influences. I extended my trust too liberally, and I made poor decisions. I lost my integrity and my identity."

He shook with desperation and anger.

Andras looked at Belial and widened his eyes, hoping Belial might have some words to escape from this downward spiral.

Belial took the cue and interjected, "Kimaris, if I may...."

Kimaris nodded, wiping his dry eyes.

"It seems that even if you have temporarily lost your identity, you have found it once again, because you are experiencing true remorse and desirous to restore the control of your own life. You must stand your ground now, set boundaries, and associate only with others who are worthy of your company."

Feeling emboldened by Belial's words, Andrealphus added his own thoughts. "Master Kimaris, I agree with Belial, and I pray for a double portion of strength upon you from the Divine Will."

Belial continued lecturing as if he had known Kimaris for years, because he saw himself in Kimaris. "True friends stimulate and sharpen each other like steel on steel. We forget our toils and inspire each other to do the same, even in the face of death!"

Andras added the question, "May we help you, Kimaris?"

"You already have," answered Kimaris, nodding his head. "Will you stay in communication?"

Andras had hoped to make this a quick visit, but now he felt confident that Kimaris could be trusted, and he liked the idea of an extended alliance. So, he proposed a communication network.

Kimaris was delighted by the idea.

"That is wonderful," beamed Kimaris. "Thank you. In for now, let me help you to reach your southern destination in the plains. From the air, you will be able to identify the area easily. I trust Officer Deanis, and I will ask him to prepare for the flight."

The foursome basked in mutual agreement and thanksgiving, feeling good about the future relationship with their new ally.

Riding upon the air, a flock of geese migrated gradually from one location to another. They had traveled quite far already, facing various vicissitudes along their journey, most recently enjoying a large feast amid the protection of large rocks along the southwestern seashore.

And now they were traveling north and arriving in the dry southern plains of Afrika. Food was scarce now, and families were separated by necessity as some went scavenging for food, sometimes never to return. But the bulk of the flock stayed huddled together and settled down in the plains.

Andras was the first to spot the geese.

Meanwhile, Glasya-Labolas and his legionnaires flew alongside, scanning the area for any threats. The area seemed safe, so they began their descent to land, and Deanis carefully lowered the balloon craft toward the ground.

"Looks like a barren wasteland!" grumbled Glasya-Labolas, floating alongside the craft. "What are we looking for here?"

But just as he finished asking the question, a sudden movement flickered in the skies over the balloon. "Heads up!" he yelled.

The balloon was never built for defensive strategy and didn't stand a chance against the fast-incoming fleet of marauders. More than thirty flying creatures boomed down from above, easily overpowering the balloon craft and the Nith-Hayachian warriors flying alongside.

Glasya-Labolas put up a fierce counterattack, knocking one of the invaders into a spin before they surrounded and subdued him. But there was no choice but to submit and hope for mercy as they overtook the craft and held the Nith-Hayach as captives.

"Surrender or die," ordered the leader of the group, who had a massive bull-like body and gryphon wings, twelve feet across. He snorted through his massive bull nose, which was pierced with a gold ring, and he hoisted his harpoon-like weapon over his shoulder into a holster.

The captives were forced to land their balloon in a small clearing on a mountainside, in a heavily wooded area. Then they were led along a trail to a well-hidden camp, which was covered by the canopy of a massive tree, firmly rooted in the mountainside, an excellent ecosystem for survival.

Spectators peered out from their tents, and some looked down from the tree, which had a network of walkways. Some of them looked like flying bulls with wings, but others had no wings.

It seemed like a small-time operation with limited means at first, but upon further observation it appeared that it had all the signs of advanced technology and refined culture, with fine structures, industry, and a central temple in the middle of the camp.

The captors paraded the captives as a sign of their dominance.

They were large and intimidating creatures with specialized metallic armor, strong blades, and deadly projectile weapons. They taunted the captives, daring them to escape so they could test the weaponry.

"Stand down, fools," ordered their leader, who preferred a more civilized outcome and was embarrassed by his crew's behavior. And yet, he was also satisfied that he was firmly in control. Then he turned to the captives.

"My name is Zagan," he said in a plain tone. "Please excuse the barbaric behavior of our crew. They fight for their lives here, and they haven't interacted with other intelligent beings like yourself in recent times. Welcome to the Heights."

"But Zagan[3], these are murderers!" seethed one of the attackers.

Belial interjected with his usual confidence. "We are not the murderers you seek, Zagan. My name is Belial of Xabuviah, and my companions and I...."

Zagan interrupted, "Calm yourselves, please. I know that you are not the murderers. I saw the assailants, and unless they use sorcery to disguise their identities, they are not among you. Besides, despite your intelligence you are much too weak and could never have killed our companion."

"Please accept...," started Belial, but Zagan cut him off again.

"He was a mighty warrior and a good husband who died while serving his duty, and he left his widow to suffer at home and malnourish her child while she grieves."

All fell completely silent.

"And as for you, strangers. Come with me to discuss further."

Zagan continued talking while they walked slowly toward the central shrine. "This morning in my spiritual study, I completed the rite of purity to commune with my ancestors, and I received a revelation from the brilliant ones who rule the glittering sphere."

The captives exchanged glances but listened closely while those in the community showed quiet respect to their King.

"I saw the division of time into periods and cycles, the heavenly settlement dividing the internal waters from the external waters, the assignment of the great lights and earthly creations into their various divisions...," Zagan trailed off, apparently caught up in a memory of the vision. He stopped walking.

Then he continued, "I saw the plants and animals reproducing upon the earth, and finally the creation of the higher beings.

"The entire creation splendid and joyous with the flaxen energy of the earth in fruition, and special beings endowed with the power to seal or unseal...." He trailed off again.

"Then I saw my own fallen state, and I felt ashamed. I have been vain in my pursuits. We have developed some practical skills and we study all the diverse magical and scientific arts... but we have lost the way.

"The angel appeared to me in a glorious form, with a body like gleaming topaz and a face of lightning, with eyes like candles burning brightly. His arms and legs shone brilliantly like newly brushed copper, and a hawk rested upon his fist. His voice rang out as many men in chorus.

"He declared the observances to me once again and foretold of your arrival."

[1] *Agares* is an old fair man, an instigator of action and language, riding upon a crocodile, and carrying a goshawk upon his fist. He has great power in his tongue to bring down spiritual and temporal edifices through earthquakes and visitations. He and his thirty-one legions teach all languages, and they prefer peace.

His eternal name and identity is יליאל (*Yelial*).

Agares-Yelial is the very same angelic personage who appeared to Daniel on multiple occasions to transmit the will of the Lord. He is an associate of the Great Prince Michael (Adam), who led the fight against the Dragon. And despite his humble appearance on the Earth as an "old fair man," in his true form he has a body which shines like topaz, a face of lightning, eyes like candles burning brightly, arms and legs shining brilliantly like copper, and a voice ringing out like voices of many men in chorus.

He is among the foremost of the אלהים (Alohim), and he declares what will occur in the last days of all times and kingdoms.

His fall was quite spectacular and noisy, a massive impenetrable tower crumbling to the ground, foreshadowing the great harm he would cause for other beings with his unbridled tongue, which is full of cursing and venomous energy.

So, his lot now is to help others. He still uses his tongue often, but in a more constructive manner.

Agares is willing to be the "bad guy" when he sees a problem, giving critical feedback when necessary, challenging a man, tearing him down before building him back up in correct form. Motivated to preserve the peace, he quells popular uprisings, and he assists to ensure victory over unjust attacks, aided by his gift of prophetic visions of the future.

His passion is quite amiable, but it can be overbearing despite his best intentions and courteous manners, so he keeps it contained and waits for the opportune moments to be most helpful.

But on occasion he fears for his precious life, and he tires from the loss of hope and meaning in life. This opposition is intense and leaves him feeling down and forsaken, so he cries out for help as David did in the 22nd Psalm:

"Deliver my soul from the sword, my precious life from the power of the dog! You, LORD, have not despised or abhorred the affliction of the afflicted, have not hidden your face from us, but have heard, when we cried to you. I will praise Him and perform my vows with due observation to those who fear You, dear Lord."

So, Agares strives to serve those who fear the Lord, and he shows faith through observances (*niyamah*):

Saucha samtosha tapah svadhyaya isvarapranidhanani, which translates to *purity, contentment, the pain of acceptance, spiritual study, and worship (self-surrender)*.

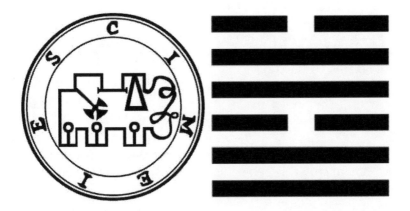

[2] In a particular part of the Earth called Afrika, a powerful and mighty marquis emerges victorious as a "valiant warrior riding upon a goodly black horse".

He has the gift of tongues, so he speaks and reasons well with good grammar, logic, and rhetoric. He commands his twenty legions of infernal spirits eloquently and succinctly, with good potential and rapport, ruling all the spirits in the parts of Afrika. His name is *Kimaris* or *Cimejes*, father of Pharaohs, worshipped by the fourth son of Ham (Canaan).

The eternal name of Kimaris is מקאליה (Manaquaeliah), whose calling is great and diverse despite his initial catastrophic fall, after which he spent many years in mourning and repentance, seeking the Lord in all earnestness as David expresses in the 38th Psalm.

His fall came after he encouraged Ham to engage in scandalous forbidden behavior to produce Egypt (literally the 'Forbidden'), the mother of Pharaoh.

He was serene with sincere inward confidence like the waters of a marsh, but he fell into complacency, giving into pleasure at the expense of his identity, so he lost himself for a time.

In conjunction with his fall, he develops some bad physical characteristics, such as epilepsy, and poor moral qualities.

He angered God and fell into a deep depression, so he felt great despair, discomfort, paranoia, and despondency, creating a hell full of enemies and mistrust, while seeking false pleasures and deliberating restlessly.

Eventually he put his trust in the one who would unintentionally and ignorantly injure him, to break the cycle.

His own strength and sincerity were insufficient alone to handle the current problems in his life, so he called out to the Lord for help and sincerely repented.

And he realized his pathetic broken state, but he also found himself still in possession of a soul and an identity.

So, his virtue was still dim, but instead of gathering around the false light of injurious influences, he began to find pleasure in being his own light, leading and attracting others to himself, seeking true joy and eternal pleasure, consisting of heartfelt ironclad determination and true integrity, within himself and among others worthy of the company.

He resolved to control and direct the placid mildness with firmness and correctness, with a double portion of strength allocated him from the divine, stabilizing with forward momentum and finding his self-worth.

His calling is introverted, but he finds true love and meaning within himself, which invites others to love as well, so he finds purpose in supporting and maintaining himself and his friends, vegetation, and aquatic animals, and he influences dreams with a gentle character.

He forgets his toils and inspires others to do the same, even in the face of death, due to the animating lift of selfless service.

The hearth of the earth burns with compassion and life.

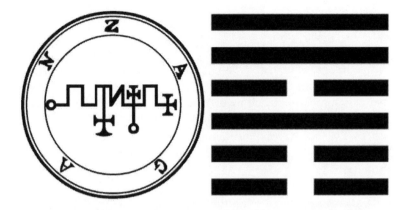

[3] Another intelligence of this earthly sphere is known as *Zagan*, the great king and president, who appears with his thirty-three legions in the form of a bull with gryphon's wings, though he eventually returned to his original angelic human personage known as ומבאל (*Ombael*), representing the God above all things.

He is witty, and he tends to evoke the same sort of wittiness in those who befriend him, along with practical magical skills in the arts and scientific procedures, such as the transmutation of matter and metallurgical arts.

His heart is sensitive, and he seeks honest pleasures, such as travel and friendships, which he fosters and encourages in others.

He helps fulfill a prophecy of Malachi about the prophet *Elijah*, who comes to seal the hearts of the parents to their children, and the children to their parents, and souls to souls as eternal mates.

So, his purpose is very good in the end, but he began his journey with a fall, due to his vices which were contrary to nature.

His deep desire for companionship led him to make some less than noble compromises.

His initial mistake was to allow the idea of liberty to corrupt into libertinism and hedonistic excesses.

But he learned from his mistakes after experiencing the results, and now he teaches fools to become wise.

His saving grace is his return to humility and sincere praise of the almighty Lord. So, as he performs his works, he is quick to speak with reverence and awe about the God above all, high up and caring for his creations with such admirable magnificence and intelligence beyond all intelligence, power beyond power, love beyond love, and total perfection. Such mercy, such grace! (Reference *Psalms 113*).

He wavers at times, but he finds strength in picking a direction, getting back on track, willing to bear his cross in his heart and accept his fate, like a snake on his belly.

He is brilliant and capable of all the glittering splendor of Venus.

The story of Zagan is one of gradual progress and advancement, like the flock of geese migrating from place to place in the story. The inexperienced young geese struggle at first, as an officer learning his calling, facing criticism, but in the end he succeeds. There are good times and bad times; time for rest and feasting, yet also time for loss and pain, such as when his brother dies while serving his duty, leaving his wife to suffer and malnourish her child. So, by necessity, he finds strength to rise above and resist further plunder amid terrible circumstances.

He had been very docile, but rage and pain welled up inside, manifesting as a fight for survival and adaptability, just as the geese land on stable branches of a tree to rest and prepare for the next phase of their journey, or when the widow finds new love and becomes pregnant again, this time to success.

So, likewise, each advancement in Zagan's life is gradual until he advances to the "large heights beyond". He has learned much and wears many feathers in his cap now, and he carries himself with quiet serenity, restful and flexible as a firmly rooted tree in the mountain. The environment is good and sustains his life, allowing virtues, firmness, and correctness (direction).

Chapter 8 – Glory

Foreword

*In the world of the forms, location is very important.
(And so is consistency.)*

*We are in the present day, in the present moment, and we are
called to enjoy the blessing of the current day and current space,
or to endure through difficulties and evils, if God allows them,
until the final beneficent result.*

*Albert Pike eloquently wrote, "The present is our scene of action,
and the future for speculation and trust; man was sent upon the
earth to live in it, to enjoy it, to study it, to love it, to embellish it,
to make the most of it. If life is worthless, so also is immortality."*

*Scientists and wisemen correctly observe that the earth is like a
microscopic droplet of water in the universal ocean, and yet in
this life let us remember that "it is the invisible and therefore
unobserved that is most beautiful."*

*And even in this droplet, all creatures and consciousness may
"feel" the divine link; "The humblest life may feel its connection
with its infinite source."*

"Thus earth, which binds many in chains, is... the starting place and goal of immortality. Many it buries in the rubbish of dull cares and wearying vanities; but to [us] it is the lofty mount of meditation where Heaven and Infinity and Eternity are spread before [us] and around [us]. To the lofty-minded, the pure..., this life is the beginning of Heaven, and a part of immortality."

In the Norse legends, Heimdall was well known for his keen sense of observation, which he used to recognize and inquire into the Truth, in all its various colors and rays, starting with each stellar light in the sky and the light of the planets.

These lights are the sons and daughters of God among angels, who lead the herald of the Lord in the heavens, then the Earth.

Heimdall felt his connection with the infinite source, and he saw his role as the Intendant of Formation, since he knew that this present life is of the utmost importance in the eternal scheme.

He chose a battle, even in the face of opposition, and he found that angels attended to and inspired his mind to greater heights, brighter lights, powerful motive force, and meditation (dhyana).

Loved by all, Heimdall is Watcher and Warder of the Rainbow, observing all the creations and guarding the Bifrost bridge, gleaming resplendently like a flash of light, possessing only his brilliant sword and the Gjallarhorn – the trumpet of warning.

He is a fierce and fearless warrior for Earth, restoring balance whenever the balance is threatened, such as when he overtook Loki to repossess the Brisingamen. Through long persistence and observation, and through gentleness like the rain and dew, he outwits the transforming tricks of Master Mayhem

---

.

As Zagan spoke about his glorious vision, a

cat jumped up onto his lap and purred. Andras noticed the cat
was especially interested in the mysterious rune necklace
hanging around his neck, and it mindlessly pawed at it.

"What are these observances of which you speak?" asked Belial.

"Ah. *Saucha samtosha tapah svadhyaya isvarapranidhanani,*"
he uttered rhythmically in a breath. "These are the observances.
They are out of our control. They are aspects of the creation.
They were taught to our forefathers by the Intermediary who
carries a hawk upon his fist."

Zagan stopped to consider, and the others exchanged glances,
wondering if this Intermediary might have been Agares or
perhaps another of the Yelial. Zagan continued reverently.

"The observances are *purity, contentment, acceptance of pain,
spiritual study, and surrender of self.*"

Glasya-Labolas paid close attention to Zagan's words, trying to
understand their meaning. And despite being mistreated earlier,
he had warmed up to Zagan now and even felt special kinship,
perhaps because their physical appearance was somewhat alike,
particularly the wings and muscular features. He spoke up next.

"Zagan, we were sent here by one who also carried a hawk on
his fist, and he told us that we might be of service to you. Let us
help you find the fugitive who killed your brother."

The others nodded in silent agreement, ready to help if possible.

Zagan nodded and beamed with gratitude. "Yes, I believe you can help. Thank you for the offer. Please. Come with me."

Zagan showed them the evidence, and the hunt was short-lived, almost anti-climactic.

Andras detected a faint trail of blood, which led to an assailant, hiding among the vast herds of cattle outside the settlement. He was easily captured and brought to justice.

The capture and prosecution of the murderer did not restore their lost brother, but it provided some closure to his widow, who was at home with their suckling child. The community was quick to offer support and love to help her during this challenging time.

They all gathered at the base of the massive central tree to perform the funeral service, where many expressed thanks and paid their respects, bearing testimonies of eternal soul life.

After the funeral service, Zagan invited Andras, Andrealphus, Glasya-Labolas, and Belial to the temple.

"Perhaps the Lord will see fit to give you counsel regarding the next phase of your journey," he offered with gratitude.

Allowing the strangers to enter the holy temple was the highest sign of respect and trust he could offer. He also offered his rune necklace to Andras as a token of his appreciation.

"This necklace is very special to me, but I have learned what it had to teach, and I am ready to pass its blessing along to you. These runes are imbued with elemental magic and allow spirits to communicate. But be cautioned to only invoke the *Holy* Spirit and use the necklace with faith. Eventually you will no longer need the necklace, but it will help you in the meantime."

Andras was honored and wore the necklace proudly, peering at the runes and multi-colored gemstones along its string.

They visited the inner chambers of the temple and were amused to see the cat once again.

She was lounging at first, then took an interest in the visitors, standing up and arching her spine, wandering over to mingle. "*Meow*," she offered. Her fur and whiskers glistened white.

The temple was constructed with fine woodwork and well lit, decorated with mirrors, tables, chairs, carvings, artwork, and a magnificent stage. The craftsmanship was exquisite.

Actors and actresses performed on the stage, enacting certain scenes from history, taking part in solemn rituals of purification. The main point of the rituals was to teach and reinforce the five main observances mentioned by Zagan:

Saucha samtosha tapah svadhyaya isvarapranidhanani.

The visitors offered solemn oaths to practice these observances, and at the end of the presentation, they spent time mingling in a special room, the most beautiful room of them all, to ponder.

And in this room, each of them experienced a vision:

The air around Andras took on a new crystalline characteristic, and he saw waves of fluctuating energy as if he was underwater, and phantoms of his worst fears filled the room to torment him.

He focused his attention on a single point in the chaotic waves, and he prayed for courage to face his fears in the ensuing doom. And soon after his prayer, he faced the most fearful phantom of them all, watching intently until it flickered to a soft white glow, and a strange man appeared before him, dressed in a white robe, with a raven's head like his own and canine teeth.

He whispered, *"Go west into the mountains,"* then disappeared.

Glasya-Labolas saw a lion with gryphon's wings like his own, protecting the mountain.

Belial saw a lake and heard thunder, then looked up and beheld a two-headed dragon high in the sky, silhouetted by the sun.

And Andrealphus couldn't speak about what he saw, but he was taken away in a blissful trance and eager to go west as well.

So, the party of sixteen left the mountain village of Omabael, traveling west, past a large body of water in the mountains. They traveled by balloon, with Nith-Hayachians on the wing.

And they ascended past the layer of mist covering the lands, never dispersing nor moving like regular clouds, but dwelling as a permanent part of the ecosystem and veiling the mountaintops like a plush velvet blanket.

The sight of the Earth below from such heights was breathtaking. The air was thin, so their breathing was more labored than usual, but they were inspired by the beauty and grandeur of the scene. And the sun seemed much closer, yet the air was freezing cold, so, many of them were shivering and sniveling despite the coats, provided by the Omabaelians.

Andras was not bothered, but rather invigorated by the cold air, and he played with the necklace he had received from Zagan, inspecting its characters, which would change from time to time. He observed the gems as they sparkled with light in response to his interactions and questions, confirming truth as he spoke.

"What is the Holy Spirit?" he wondered aloud to himself.

Then he returned his gaze to the snow-capped mountains and felt mystified by the scene. He had flown many times as a raven and seen many sights from high up in the air, which was always inspiring but never quite this impressive. Those days of flying fast with wings were long gone now, since he gave up his wings and became a man with hands to build tools, towns, and so on.

He missed the skies, and he felt grateful for the balloon to float in the air once again, albeit much slower.

A rainbow appeared high above the highest peak, adding to the mystique as it appeared to touch down on the mountain.

Deanis looked at Andras and Belial, still fixed on the rainbow, and pointed down to a clearing where they could land.

And they nodded in approval, so he began to lower the craft.

On the ground, they surveyed the land and quickly located the mouth of a cavern.

It seemed like it might make a good temporary shelter, so they agreed to explore inside.

But before they could enter while still assembling themselves, they heard a faint sound which filled the air on all sides with a soft yet permeating resonance, and a brilliant light filled the air as two luminous forms emerged from the cavern.

The first was a wolf with a serpentine tail, flames in his mouth, and the second was a lion with gryphon's wings.

The former then assumed the form of a man with a raven's head, like the appearance of Andras, but with wolfish teeth, just as Andras had seen in his vision. He was strong and powerful, yet calm and serene, comfortable with the arrival of the visitors. His eyes were brilliant and yellowish white in color, and his body gleamed resplendently like a flash of light, blinding the visitors until their vision adjusted to the stunning brilliance.

Along his right hip hung his sheathed sword, but he showed no signs of hostility. He smiled and exposed his sparkling teeth.

Once their eyes adjusted to the brighter light, they noticed many more details all around, including an elaborate entryway behind the man into the cavern, and a dazzling array of light and color emanating from within, like a swirling prismatic mist that highlighted the crystalline features of the granite.

Andrealphus could hardly bear the light and covered his eyes, barely peeking through his shaky fingers.

"Greetings. My name is Amon-Akayah," the being of light stated with a harmonious ring in his voice, then pointed to the lion with gryphon's wings and said, *"And this is my best student, Napula. How may we assist you?"*

His tone was far-off and aloof, rested and relaxed and peaceful, as if he knew his place perfectly.

He wasted no movements, gliding with grace and elegance at the proper time, with brilliant intelligence, in a perfect union with the entire mountain and the whole Earth.

He had been observing the visitors and expected their arrival.

Belial had the courage to speak:

"We are on a quest of discovery and were guided to this place by our Higher Power. We seek knowledge and new friendships to build the kingdom. May we enter your domain and learn more?" he asked sincerely.

Amon[1] smiled again with his gleaming teeth, looked around at each of them, then continued distantly, *"Ah, the energy of youth, ruled by the primal physical body and its passions."*

Then he sighed with an aloof look and his eyes glowed even whiter than before. "It's been a long and interesting process of self-discovery. I see that you are also on the path."

Curious and wanting to learn more, Glasya-Labolas asked, "Which path?"

"Come with me and I will explain," Amon replied, motioning with his head and turning back toward the brilliant cavern.

The inside of the cave was brilliant and ornate, with angular arched designs and polished surfaces of gleaming granite, leading up to a large doorway. Amon unsheathed his sword, turned to the doorway, and wielded the sword with the tip down, gripping the hilt with both hands.

The sword had a key-like pattern at the end of the blade, with special notches, grooves, and markings. He held up the sword, placed its tip in a slot near the base of the door, and turned it to open the doorway.

The inner chamber was guarded by a group of creatures that resembled Napula[2], lions with large wings. And they stood immobile but very observant.

The room was domed and spacious, with a skylight overhead, and an archway at the end which appeared to lead out into the open rainbow-colored sky. Colors were dazzling and hypnotic, slowly changing hues and sparkling like diamonds.

"Over the precipice lies a portal to the sky kingdom known as Yehahael, where Volak rules. You will meet him, but first...."

None of the visitors were doubtful nor afraid of Amon or Napula in the slightest. Somehow, due to Amon's soothing speech and the astounding presentation of lights and wonders, they were completely ready to listen and proceed. Some of them stepped toward the archway automatically, as if they were compelled to move forward without thinking.

"Stop."

So, they stopped at Amon's command, snapped out of the trance, and shook their heads in surprise.

"You have good intentions, but you have much to learn about yourselves and the world," he commented. Then he smiled again and continued. "Reminds me of myself in my younger days, totally unaware of my toes and my brain, unable to really find rest or peace in my soul, moving around without a purpose."

He straightened his stance and his eyes seemed to wander, recalling memories, viewing a far-away place with second sight.

But then he snapped back into the present, and he continued, *"The beginning of true self-awareness and meditation begins with the combination of rest and unrest. You can calm yourself, but then further excitement boils up from within, tearing at the heart until it burns...."*

Andras felt his own heart begin to burn as he listened, and he looked at the others and saw they were feeling the same anxiety, rustling with an anxious energy.

Was it something in the air?

"Stop," he commanded again with a wave of his right hand, sensing their discomfort. *"Arrest your senses and take a close look at this mindlessness that you feel inside. Do you feel it?"*

They nodded, and he continued. *"Good. This feeling of unrest is the beginning of what we call the Mind. Stress and discomfort create awareness, and so, we form a resolution to take control, set limits, and separate our conscious choices from the continual autonomous motion all around us."*

Amon breathed deeply and slowly, and the others followed suit.

"Feel the toes and calves, then the legs and loins, the ribs and scapulae, the spine and shoulders and wings, the heart...."

He paused to feel his heart, and all the others followed his lead.

Then he continued. *"The arms and fingers and jawbone, and even the words of our mouths.... See?"*

They all nodded, many of them with their eyes closed now.

The energy in the air was palpable, vibrating with a continuous pulse that generated an audible sequence of tones, each new tone adding to the others as the room became brighter and brighter, until a brilliant flash filled the room.

Andrealphus and some others fainted to the ground.

Andras looked around in confusion, still blinded by the light but barely able to make out the forms of his companions.

His vision and other senses began to sharpen, yet everything seemed strange and misshapen, as if they were surrounded by prisms distorting the light in every direction. He tried to move and felt numb, then realized they were apparently suspended in the air, high above a lake. He heard some rumbling, but the sound was muffled as if his ears were covered with thick glass.

He realized the sound must have come from the nearby clouds, thick and dark. It must have been thunder, he thought.

But as he turned to locate the source of the thunderous sound, suddenly his perspective changed, and he was inside the cloud.

A panic took over, but he remembered the guidance of Amon and regathered his mind within himself, with deep and relaxed breathing until he could see his companions again.

His companions looked as if they were made of triangles and other shapes, sometimes shifting or disappearing.

"This is the dimension of Yehahael," said Amon, "where Volak[3] resides, moving quickly and searching the depths."

Hearing the voice of Amon was reassuring and helped the group gather their wits about them, despite the unusual vantage point. Somehow the new dimension made sense to Andras intuitively, so he accepted this as a new place, not merely a state of mind, but a *place* outside his normal world.

This must be where the angels roam, he thought.

Volak came suddenly in a flash of light, accompanied by a thunderous rumble, appearing as a young child with wings, riding upon a two-headed dragon.

"I saw this in the temple of Zagan," said Belial. "I was here!"

"*Hello brother*," said the child with a friendly demeanor.

"Hello Volak," Amon answered with his tenor voice, then took the opportunity to introduce the strangers. "How is your quest?"

"Not so well really," Volak answered calmly. "But well enough."

"Well enough?"

"I fought fiercely against the heinous serpents, and I suffered an attack which left me blind in one eye, now healing very slowly, but I can see with the other, and the battle was a success overall. We found many wonderful treasures and many more lie in wait. Thankfully I was well protected by my legions."

Despite his childlike appearance, Volak was an old soul whose age and experience showed in his expression and mannerisms.

"What happened with your marriage proposal?" asked Amon.

"It was not the right time," Volak answered with disappointment. "I live the life of a solitary widow, yet I feel strong in resolve."

He seemed to struggle with the thought, but continued in his effeminate voice, "I battle with the serpents, yet I enjoy peace, and I serve the mortals, those who seek light and love wisdom."

"Volak, how long will you allow your past to control you?" asked Amon, with apparently deep concern. "You deserve much more than this. You've repented of your sins and regained trust. What keeps you here in this realm?"

Volak swallowed and strained to speak, and then he whispered, "The one I love is still trapped by his enemies."

Amon shook his head with disappointment.

"I will pursue her until I succeed, or until I am finally dead."

"Volak, please," said Amon. "The one you seek is out of reach, and she is not right for you."

"Silence, brother!" Volak retorted with a squeak.

Amon lowered his head, realizing he could not persuade Volak, and he looked at the others for help.

Andras realized that this must be the reason Amon had brought them here, to help save his sibling from this alternate dimension, which Amon considered to be a prison.

But Volak went on, "You want to change me, and you brought your friends to save me, but you have wasted your time, brother. I know what I want, and I found a humble life with a connection to the Infinite. What else could I want? Immortality and eternal life begin here and now, within the bounds of this reality."

"Yes," replied Amon, "and just as our father taught us, the Earth is the great starting place, the mount of meditation. But you left the Earth and joined this other... dimension, in search of the...."

Volak sighed, and the dragon shook its two heads under him, apparently feeling his frustration and his desire to start moving.

Then he continued, "Eventually I may return to the Earth realm, my brother, but for now please accept that I have chosen a different location. Will you also try to pry our eternal father back from his heavenly realm? Shouldn't we trust in him to conduct his life as he pleases, and patiently await the change? There is evil in this realm just as there is evil upon the Earth, but I trust our father's counsel, that the good will prevail."

Amon looked around at the others, but they had nothing to offer. This issue was far beyond their current knowledge to comment.

So, he turned to Volak and conceded with a nod, but remarked, "I will not give up on you, my dear Volak. I do remember our father's counsel often, that we ought to look for Truth in all its various colors and arrays. Perhaps we both take after our father in various ways...."

His eyes burned brilliantly as spoke, and he looked up to the sky and pointed toward the prismatic Sun. "There he is among the mercurial heat of the Sun. Somehow, he maintains his integrity and uniformity in regular revolutions around the scorching Sun, there with the other angels who herald and prepare for the Lord of the heavens and earth to return once again. We all have our places in the grand scheme, but I hope you know that I love you, and I welcome you back to the Earth any time."

He paused, then continued. "If our father were here right now, he would be proud of us and tell us to choose our battles wisely, standing bravely in the face of opposition. He would turn our minds to the angels who attend us and inspire our minds toward greater heights, greener pastures, and brighter light. He would remind us that this Earth is a child of the Infinite creation, and the center of meditation."

"Goodbye, Volak. Please signal if you ever need my help."

They departed as quickly as they had arrived, reappearing back in the mountains, suddenly feeling very heavy and awkward.

Andras moved his hand back and forth to test his body and reassure himself that they were back in the physical realm.

Amon was disappointed, but he smiled and thanked the travelers. "Perhaps we all learned something today," he said with a distant look in his brilliant eyes again. "I also started in ignorance and rejected the truth, and only over time I stopped fighting and began to accept the truth. What once required effort has now become effortless, but it seems the effort was never wasted."

He took two vials from his workbench and peered into them. One was filled with crystalline-blue liquid; the other was empty. He poured the contents from one to the other, then back again, and repeated the cycle a few more times without thinking or paying close attention, feeling distracted.

[1] Among the formations of God on this Earth, one entity appears as a wolf with a serpent's tail, spewing flames from his mouth, then transforming into the form of a man with a raven's head, still retaining the teeth of a canine.

Forty legions of spirits follow the Marquis, who is stern and great in power, knowledgeable about all things past and to come, and able to mend relationships or resolve controversies with his wisdom. His name is אמון (*Amon*), or properly אכאיה (*Akayah*).

Akayah fell and became known as Amon because he felt slighted by others and rebelled against sure knowledge. He was destined to become a son of perdition without hope for eternal exaltation, but ultimately, he relearns patience and his good heart prevails. He remembers how to communicate and trust the Spirit again. He loves learning and accomplishing the most challenging tasks.

And now he praises the Lord with all his soul, grateful for his mercy and grace, his patience and love, his continual restoration and renewal of life. He finds new love and feels a renewed vigor and energy well up within him, which provokes dedication to the Lord and a willingness to love and emulate his beneficence. (Reference *Psalms 103*.)

But he has quite a struggle of acceptance in a severe test of his patience before he arrives at this point.

He'd like to solve all the world's problems at once, starting with his own selfish interests and pursuits, but he realizes that this isn't the proper order of things, and before he can move forward, he must go back and study and re-learn to meditate.

In the *Book of Mormon*, we meet Ammon, a strong and mighty Mulekite (of David's lineage) who was pivotal in uniting the scattered remnants of the Nephites. He was not always faithful, but he eventually came to believe that the Nephite King Mosiah was a prophet and seer. He and his companions accepted the assignment from King Mosiah to find the lost people of Zeniff, who strayed from the Nephites three generations before.

The assignment was very difficult, described as forty days of "hunger, thirst, and fatigue," only to be captured and imprisoned by the Zeniffites when they finally found the place. But Ammon quickly gains the trust of King Limhi (the descendant of both Zeniff and the evil king Noah), and they all return to Zarahemla, where the Zeniffites gladly accept the leadership of King Mosiah and the prophet Alma, overjoyed to escape the subjection of the Lamanites. Ammon was an instrument in the hands of the Lord.

The second Ammon appears shortly thereafter, one generation younger than the first, and the same story almost repeats itself. This younger Ammon is a son of King Mosiah, and he rebelled against sure knowledge in his youth. But he and his brethren (and Alma the Younger) were miraculously visited by an angel and became strong proponents of the faith. And like the former Ammon, he also accepted a mission from the same King Mosiah, once again to the land of Nephi, but this time to the Lamanites. The journey was arduous, and when Ammon arrived in Ishmael, he was bound with cords and presented to the Lamanite King.

And like the first, this Ammon was an instrument in the hands of the Lord. He offered to serve the King and mightily defended the Lamanites from robbers. His feats were so astounding that King Lamoni believed he was the legendary Great Spirit, but Ammon explained he was merely a man who was inspired by the Holy Ghost, acting as an instrument in the hands of God.

And through his service and his words, many of the Lamanites were inspired to listen, repent, and convert to the Christian faith.

[2] *Napula*, sometimes called *Vapula*, is the strong and mighty Duke who fell and appears on the Earth most often as a lion with gryphon's wings, governing thirty-six legions of spirits.

He is known in the eternities by his name מצראל (*Mizrael*), who is particularly gifted in the art of comforting the oppressed.

His past is marked with a streak of insubordination, but over time he learned to comfort the oppressed, cure mental illness, and deliver the persecuted to safety, longevity, and virtuosity.

He needed to relearn the lesson of slowing down, taking rest, and finding a steady state. He was moving fast with good intentions, but without really using his brain or any serious, critical thought. Instead, he allowed his life to be ruled by more primal instincts of the physical body in its diverse gyrations.

The first step in the process was to feel his *toes* and let them rest. They had taken quite a beating over the years from overactivity because he treated them like objects rather than a part of himself.

He gained greater awareness, but he was still frustrated and followed others haphazardly, with great mental dissatisfaction.

So, he paid attention to each part of his body, up into his spine, which was sore from his previous poor posture. He straightened his stance and began listening more carefully to stay in balance. But he still felt more unrest and excitement within his heart, which surged and strained with great stress.

The turmoil created a perilous situation in which the heart began to burn with strong repressed emotions, leading to violence and senseless acts of stupidity. So eventually, after painful lessons, he knew he needed to *stop* at a limit and *separate* his Inner Eye from the continual autonomous motion all around.

So, he gained greater awareness and resolution, but he was still unconsciously suffocating himself with his shallow breathing, which was causing his heart to scream for oxygen. He gasped desperately for air, and his lungs heaved wildly, irregularly at first, until eventually he re-learned to breathe deeply and rest.

Along with this restfulness came greater awareness of his words and his jawbone, and relaxation throughout all his facial features. And finally, all occasion for regret disappeared, and orderliness returned to his mind, words, and actions.

He felt weak and divided in a sense, yet in harmony with his surroundings and his positioning. His will was swallowed up in the virtue of the Holy One, so he felt no urge to speak rashly or impose upon others.

He rested and waited patiently like a generous mountain (*kăn*), knowing his place and his principles, and losing his identity in the consciousness of the whole, moving and resting at the proper time with brilliance and intelligence.

[3] *Volak* is a mighty president, distinguished by his high office, organization, and childlike appearance, governing thirty-eight legions in his Eastern domain.

He has cherubic wings and often rides high upon a two-headed dragon, so he can identify serpents and hidden treasures below, and he offers true answers to the sincere seeker of truth without being forced or provoked.

He is the fallen nature of the supreme being known as *Suna*, or more properly יההאל (*Yehahael*).

With great power, high status, and a life of luxurious comforts, he was tempted like David, which led to scandal and betrayal, causing a rift in trust within himself and among others, and he became emasculated as a result.

He would spend the rest of his physical life in desperate song, pleading with the Lord for forgiveness and protection.

Despite the turmoil and his guilty conscience, he loved wisdom, and he inspired others to acquire wisdom, founding philosophy and the branch of brothers known as the *Illuminati*.

He prefers the tranquility of solitude over pomp and fanfare, but his followers love to be in his presence because he is modest and nonthreatening, peace-loving, and virtuous.

The only thing that disgusts and angers Volak is faithlessness. His was a crime of passion, but he never lost faith in the Lord. But when he becomes angry with faithless enemies, he is quick to refocus on his own faults and seek forgiveness, admitting his complete reliance upon the Lord and his precepts for salvation. He speaks directly to him in his prayers and with songs, poems, and writings, with a love for the truth and enduring testimony. (Reference *Psalms 119:139.*)

His guilt and emasculation led him to seek an ancillary position in marriage, usually seeking a strong masculine counterpart to master and rule over his house, since he doubted his own ability. He felt unworthy to experience pleasure for himself, but he felt great satisfaction when he could provide service for his master.

So, he waited patiently upon his master like a solitary widow, maintaining firm correctness in proper form, accepting his fate, and improving his abilities.

Eventually he gained the full favor of his master and became the primary servant, which caused great unrest in the kingdom as if a princess was upstaged by her youngest sister at the wedding.

But the relationship was out of balance because he had sought his master instead of waiting for his master to seek him instead. It was an empty offering, like a bloodless sacrifice, as if the Earth tried to initiate a relationship with Heaven rather than Heaven initiating with the Earth. His desires were sincere but out of order, so disparity of age and wisdom caused confusion. Heaven did respond, with thunder rolling over the marsh with powerful movement, but this was not the desire of the Earth.

So, the Earth was forced to re-accept the ancillary position, lesser bride of the Heavens, but it also flourished with growth. They began to communicate honestly, which caused discomfort at first, but his *going* became *giving in*, and balance was restored naturally toward the proper ordering of things.

Chapter 9 – Foundation

Foreword

"As there is but one heaven, so there is but one earth."
—Unknown

The Earth is among the deepest mysteries, beyond metaphors.

She is the goddess of fertility known in the legends as Nerthus, the Queen of the Vanir, who is "strong, vigorous, and healthy," perfectly obedient to the Lord, the bringer of peace, and the foundation for life. As her fires blaze deeply with omnipotence, she offers herself to any worthy hand, a grand coach to contain her most valuable passengers, providing the finest of all linens and the richest of all soils.

Her personalities are many, but she stands firm like the heifer, calmly and serenely minding her sphere and rotation perfectly, resting in tacit firmness. Her infinite capacity is the definition and goal of all fortune.

She receives the influences of the Heavens with near perfection. She supports and contains all, waits patiently for direction from the Lord, and advocates for her children as well as is possible, with wide comprehension and great brightness.

She can move like the mare, and does so gracefully with tender mildness and docility, yet firmness leading to great good fortune.

The manifestations of the earth are diverse and multifaceted, from the hoarfrost signaling the onset of winter to the greatness and exactitude of an edifice or temple. She demonstrates her excellence under restraint, firmly maintained. She is docile like a garment, specially endowed to cover the generative force of the Spirit, receiving favors and good fortunes from the same. Her dragons rise from the fields and fight in the wild, with drops of purple and yellow blood to fertilize her fields, regenerating a new crop, and filling the air with the essence of life.

The Earth has mastered samyama (integration), which consists of dharana (concentration) and dhyana (meditation), and finally the pinnacle of samadhi (meditative consciousness), whereby certain powers are gained with respect to prakriti (nature) and her gunas (strands) – sattva (balance and harmony), rajas (activity and passion), and tamas (inertia).

As described in the Yoga Sutras of Patanjali and expounded by Satchidananda, the most significant catch of all is the "Self-ish", and the mind of the same. How does one gain knowledge of the selfish mind and her mind stuff? Through samyama on the heart. Which leads to the original sutra and the purpose of yoga:

Yoga chitta vritti nirodhah
(Yoga is the restraint of the modifications of the mind stuff).

Such requires an understanding of one's identity as the Watcher, who is One with Purusha and Divine Self abiding in all beings. From samadhi, all afflictions and karma cease.

Certain siddhis (powers and accomplishments) will be attained along the way, supernatural as they are, blocking or delaying nirbija (seedless) samadhi, but advancing us in the temporal and worldly pursuits, which is also noble. This is the process of knowing oneself and one's domains, powers, and callings, and reconnecting to the Earth.

These powers may include shrinking or growing, changing density, traveling, achieving desires, creating, commanding, controlling, and so on.

The focus of samyama is often on the relationships, such as the relationship between the ear and ether, or the body and ether, the sahasrara chakra (the light at the crown of the head), intellect and the Purusha (sometimes called Atman or Self), etc., by which all knowledge may be attained.

There's a reason why the well-disposed Eumenides were nicknamed the Furies, and futility connects to pure primal rage. It becomes important for the magician and scientist to embrace, rather than deny such feelings or spirits, and then tame them for the greater good.

We will now meet Barbatos, Buer, and Haures.

Amon took a seat in his mountain throne, surrounded by Napula and his legion of silent winged lions, which peacefully monitored the situation. He continued pouring the crystalline-blue liquid back and forth between the two vials, then fell into his trance of second sight once again, leaving the others to wonder whether they ought to interrupt his reverie.

Maybe it was time to leave?

Then he snapped back into reality and approached the doorway, using his sword-key to open the door, leading out toward the mouth of the cavern. And as he opened the door, a small dog came running into the room, excitedly wagging its tail.

Glasya-Labolas was startled at first, and he readied for battle with the invader, but Amon raised his hand to calm his nerves and smiled brightly.

"Hello, my little friend!" Amon expressed with exuberance, forgetting all about Volak for a moment as he scratched the dog.

Everyone in the room felt their joy, which lightened the mood. Smiles could be seen all around.

Then Amon turned back to the group. "My friends, I feel a debt of gratitude to you. I know there is special kinship in our future. Volak and I will need to stay in our domains, but I offer our armies to your service."

"Armies?" questioned Belial, still the most assertive.

"Yes indeed," Amon answered seriously, then pointed around to the winged lion guards. "Each of these generals commands a legion of ten or more thousand, and we will take up arms in defense of your cause."

"What did you have in mind?" asked Glasya-Labolas weakly. "Some sort of trade agreement or mutual-protection pact?"

"We have no need for protection, for we are highly capable warriors who have dominion over the lands. We have been watching you for quite some time, and I feel your cause is just. We can provide for ourselves, but if you will build roads or some other trade network between our lands, then we will be interested to trade some goods back and forth. We will send our warriors to your land if you help feed and care for them; assist them in the development of outposts. They will secure the land and ensure you will have the freedom to develop your temple and other enterprises in the land."

The travelers all exchanged glances and nods. Normally they would take a private conference to discuss and debate the details, but in this case the feeling was automatically unanimous.

Andras spoke as the spokesman for the kingdom of Mahashiah:

"Worthy Amon, your offer is most gracious, and we will accept, but I have some questions about implementation. We are set upon building the temple in our primary land, called Mahashiah. We have learned much from the Aornaelians and Omabaelians about temples and observances, and my teacher Amdusias also taught me much in the ways of communing with our God."

He continued, "Your protection is valuable, but our economy will be strained to support such a large number of warriors, so we will need them to assist in the industry of the land, to build new mines and take part in the production of goods, and to build this network of roads and so on."

"Say no more," Amon responded. "These warriors are the finest sort of workers. When they are not engaged in battle, they will participate as some of the most productive, respectable citizens in your civilization. They also understand the chain of command and government very well. They were born guardian watchers, so they will keep each other in check."

Glasya-Labolas was somewhat suspicious and worried now, thinking about the massive management problem this creates, along with potential questions about allegiance and authority. "Perhaps we should only take on a single regiment for now and integrate them as the first wave to set a precedence," he offered.

Andras liked the idea, and they began hashing out details of how many could come with the first wave, and when they would be ready for the second.

Belial had become a full partner and a leader in their fellowship, yet he had not visited Mahashiah, so he deferred to others and agreed to help with management however possible. He also offered to take a second group of Napula's warriors, known as Mizraelians, up in his homeland of Xabuviah. His eyes lit up with fiery excitement as he spoke about the possibilities.

"Amon, what's in it for you?" asked Glasya-Labolas frankly.

"Ah yes," Amon started, obviously aware that this question might come up. "Despite the mightiness of my armies, I have my concerns about the kingdom of Aychael in the northlands. You can help us to surround and control this problem before it spreads and begins to infect our lands. Ever since Amdusias began to consort and do business with the Haaiahan dragons...."

Andras, Andrealphus, and Glasya-Labolas exchanged glances after Amon mentioned Amdusias.

"You heard Volak speak about the serpents he had slain...," Amon started and trailed off, then continued, "well, these interdimensional serpents are mischievous and control the minds of certain Haaiahans, who in turn have created a secret cabal of lies and corruption in the center of that civilization. Bune is aware of the problem, but he believes he has it all under control, as does Orias, the Herahaelian who leads the seaport city...."

He trailed off again, as he realized the listeners weren't familiar with some of the details. Andras had long since departed ways with Amdusias, and he wasn't aware of many of the details of that civilization, including the city of Samigina and Amdusias's new companions there.

"Andras," said Amon, nodding to Andras, "had a relationship with Amdusias, and you have occupied key lands to the north, which will give us a decisive advantage when dealing with Amdusias and his expanding kingdom. Amdusias still seeks to do good, but the corruption has grown and will overtake the land if we do not brace up to protect ourselves and offer our services to save that civilization."

Andras was confused and skeptical, but he felt trust for Amon. He thought about the letter he had received from Amdusias, and the possibility of working together with Amdusias once again.

So, Andras said, "I have had a long history with this Amdusias. I left his kingdom many years ago to establish my own kingdom, but he has attempted to contact me and reconcile our efforts. Perhaps we can work together for our mutual benefit."

Amon smiled, and his dog wagged its tail with excitement as all the others nodded in agreement. The sixteen travelers and Deanis agreed to prepare for the journey and depart in the morning.

Rather than flying over the north kingdom of Aychael to return to Mahashiah, they decided to return by the roundabout passage by which they had come, touch base in Afrika and visit Zagan and Kimaris, then travel back through Belial's homeland before returning to Mahashiah. Part of the objective was to lay the groundwork and set instructions to the armies of workers, technicians, and engineers along the way to establish the roads and a communication network.

Andrealphus was excited on the return flight, emoting about the wonderful possibilities ahead and the great advantage they had, especially due to otherworldly support from Amon and Volak. The others were mostly quiet but quite amused by his rhetoric, especially considering he had passed out before they traveled into the alternate dimension to meet Volak. But Andrealphus ignored their chiding and went on about their "glorious fortune." They all felt a special sense of peace and security after their recent encounters with Amon, Napula, and Volak, strengthened and prepared for whatever would come next.

Zagan and Kimaris were overjoyed to see the travelers again, and pledged their support as well, in the form of additional armies and workers to set up a network of support and trade.

Zagan was pleased to learn about their trip and additional allies in the western mountains over the waters. He offered additional support in the skies surrounding the eastern mountains, and he agreed to secure the eastern lands and allow free passage to workers from the north, those from the house of Kimaris or others from the lands of Mahashiah who knew the passphrase.

Kimaris was overjoyed to see his first officer Deanis once again, and his demeanor had improved greatly since their first visit. The curse of the Great House had been lifted to some degree, and they had made heroic efforts to purify and strengthen the House of the Forbidden Land, taking on projects of mining, building, lawmaking, and so on.

As they traveled further north to the valley of the lake, Andras remembered the encounter with Agares, when he first appeared as a man riding upon a crocodile with a goshawk upon his fist. He felt confident they had fulfilled their mission and provided the necessary service to Kimaris and Zagan, which was now an ongoing mission of cooperation that would surely lead to victory.

They continued traveling north to the land of Xabuviah, the homeland of Belial. There, they lodged and enjoyed the mead and hydromel once again, taking time to relax, clear their minds, and exchange stories with the locals.

They were pleased to learn that some of the spy-scouts which they had sent to Goro-Paimona were successful in espionage, stealing some of the secrets of technology from the great city of the north in the Haziaelian valley. They learned more efficient ways to harness and store energy and to transmit signals through the air like magic, using special equipment to send and receive small vibrations over vast distances. One scout demonstrated this new technology, and Andras realized that his special rune necklace from Zagan might use a similar principle to operate.

"So simple, but what a mystery!" he mused to himself.

Meanwhile Amdusias left the management of Samigina to Orias, the mighty Herahaelian who strikes fear into those around him. The business of shipbuilding and many other industries were thriving in the city, but the poor folk were slaves to the rich and subjected themselves to terrible depravity to survive. The rich were proud and thought it was entertaining to employ the poor to serve them, and the poor were desperate enough to comply.

Most of the inhabitants of Samigina engaged in riotous games and gambling, and they defiled their bodies through every sort of vain ritual and false sacrament. Bune and his men were eager participants in the wild revelry. They pretended they were gods, and used forms of divination, sorcery, and superstition to puff themselves up, making a mockery of all things holy as they pretended to enact the ancient customs and rituals of sacrifice and communion, as if they were designed to enslave the weak and empower the rich.

They drank strong drink to levity and drunkenness, and they smoked strange fire in their censers, caring very little for the welfare of their brothers and sisters, or even themselves.

Their civilization, which was once great and unified in a common purpose, was beginning to crumble around the edges and corrupt within its heart.

Yet they somehow maintained the semblance of an orderly society in many respects, with laws and customs to support industrialists, merchants, scientists, and government institutions. Individuals were encouraged to become educated, learn the sciences and arts, become gainfully employed, or serve in the great military. They built strong barracks and fortresses along the border of Mahashiah and the southern border with Akayah, and they pushed further into the southwestern farmlands and canyons to extend their power and control, forcefully arresting sympathizers of their enemies.

They upheld laws and order in the name of peace and tranquility, and there were many good citizens in the land, but criminals gained power in the shadows and rose to powerful positions in the government, controlling the people through the threat of force and domination.

Amdusias himself enjoyed a good life in the southwestern lands of Aychael, where he remained pure and dealt with the concerns of his people, while Orobas raised new generations of strong equine stock, and Malthus-Agla served as a constant companion and friend to Amdusias in these trying times. They lived a good simple life full of service, traveling from township to township, organizing efforts to strengthen the hearts of the people.

Without the efforts of Amdusias, Orobas, and Malthus-Agla, strengthening the core of the communities and the hearts of the people in these lands, the fine kingdom of Aychael would have crumbled to the ground in filth and corruption, ruled only by fear and intimidation.

One of the insidious methods of control used by corrupt leaders was a form of sorcery and a false priesthood invented by men. The participants purchased and partook of a mind-numbing sacrament and indulged in various rituals to feel enlightened. These sacraments were strictly controlled by a hierarchy of men whose sole aim was to control the masses for selfish purposes.

Those who served as leaders in the public organization pretended to be friendly with each other, only if it was mutually beneficial. But even these figureheads were ignorant about the true source and center of control in this game they played. They were too numb to care.

Amdusias traced the corruption back to its source. He pretended to partake in the false sacraments and rituals, and he purchased their wares in increasing quantities. He pretended to have a vast distribution network, and eventually he gained the trust of a drug lord named Sanomon, who informed him that the primary source of these customs came from Barbatos, southwest of Aychael.

Amdusias preferred to focus on the nobler and brighter aspects of life, but he realized the importance of this mission, so he carried it out in secrecy.

Only Malthus-Agla and Orobas aware of his plans.

So, they traveled with a group of twelve to the lands of Barbatos, which was mostly an agricultural society in the deep countryside. The autumn had arrived, so the farmers were out in their fields, harvesting crops in large quantities, while thousands of cattle were grazing in the prairies. Dogs were barking as they helped shepherd the cattle and other animals, and birds were singing pleasantly as they flew around and perched along the fences or bathed in puddles.

It was hard to believe that such a peaceful and idyllic land could be the source of so much turmoil back in their own land, but the trail was clear. Their next stop was to meet with one, whom they called a 'king' in the center of the land, to make a large purchase of the narcotic sacrament they called Bhang. There were many herbs and spices sold underground as fodder for ritual sorcery, but this was the most popular and pervasive.

They learned from locals that there were four kings in the land, known as the Kings of Kehethael. They also learned of a great mysterious Duke named Barbatos[1], who ruled over the kings.

The people in the land were unostentatious, simply minding their business and staying close to the Earth, well-grounded, secure, and humble in their approach. Amdusias and the others had to ask for directions a few times, and found they were warm, pleasant, and helpful, despite a tough and gruff outer appearance.

The women appeared to run the households, tending to children and the various tasks of preparing food or washing laundry, while the men and boys performed the hard labor in the fields. Some of them sang songs of praise as they worked, or from their porches while they took a break with the family.

"Praise the One who created the night and days...
... Who mastered the depths and heights of the Earth,
... the seas and dry lands that He made!
Let us keep a heart full of song and praise...
... Lest we fall into darkness and squander our birth;
... Much better for us to do as He bade!"

"Could these people really be the source of all our ills?"
wondered Amdusias aloud to his companions.

He was impressed that they seemed to want to keep the Creator
of the Earth in the center of their minds and worship.

He continued by asking rhetorically, "Could such selfless service
really be at the heart of such corruption in our land?"

They finally arrived at the plantation where they were supposed
to meet one of the kings of Kehethael, and they were met by an
armed security detail at the fence.

One of the officers approached and asked about their business,
and Amdusias stated simply, "We have business with the king."
Then he whispered an additional password to the same guard,
which he had received from Sanomon, *"Aladiah"*.

The guard was satisfied but still on guard with his weapon ready.
The other officers were talking casually, going out of their way
to seem relaxed yet also observing the interchange cautiously.

"You can come with me," he said to Amdusias, "but the others will wait outside."

Amdusias had prepared for this scenario and responded quickly. "I need my companion to accompany us," he demanded while gesturing to Malthus. "He helps me keep track of the stock and financial matters. The others will stay outside."

The officer exchanged glances with one of his peers, then said, "We'll need to search your bags and clothing."

Amdusias sighed heavily, playing into the part of a businessman who didn't have time for such antics. "Make it quick, please."

The guards quickly patted down Amdusias and Malthus, apparently only looking for weapons, and cleared them to enter.

The complex was massive. multitiered, and deep underground. And as they walked along the corridor, they peered downward through large glass panes to the factory floor, well-organized, with machines to assist the workers in a long winding assembly line as they prepared packages for delivery. The workers wore full-body suits to protect them from inhaling the Bhang dust.

Eventually they arrived on an upper level where management personnel were inspecting the business, calling out to workers, managing orders, and talking to each other.

The managers were dressed in professional-looking attire, and they seemed to be very respectful to the guests, some of them nodding and smiling with deference as they passed.

Finally, around the corner came a man, bright-eyed, well-dressed and groomed, energetic and ready to discuss business matters. He was an older man with a full head of thick silver hair and bushy eyebrows to match, and he was very open, unassuming, and unafraid to talk freely about the product.

"You can see that we're here to prepare the finest Bhang product in the world, my friends. No secrets, no shady business, just the best product, and we care about our customers," the man said. "Sanomon said you were coming and speaks very highly of you, so I'm eager to sit down and start to make plans if you are."

Amdusias and Malthus smiled and nodded respectfully in turn. "Yes sir, I am Amdusias, and this is my companion Malthus. And you must be the king?"

The man smiled back and interrupted, "Call me Buer, if you will. I am the son of Barbatos and not a big fan of titles, but yes, I am the president of this organization."

Amdusias had expected a shady cartel that was ruled by high anxiety and suspicion, trying to hide themselves in the shadows with heavy artillery on the perimeter, but in fact, beyond the simple security check at the gate, this business of refining and packaging Bhang was respectable and entirely professional.

Amdusias also was impressed with Buer[2] and curious to learn more about this enigmatic character.

"You see," said Buer, "the Bhang is just a symbol and a vehicle which can be used for both good and bad. I know many use it for the wrong purposes, to invite the wrong spirits in their lives, but the plant is like any life form, with a soul and intelligence, willingness to survive and communicate, and to learn and teach. The artistry of the plant is amazing and speaks as a testimony of the Creator, and it has helped heal many souls who are ready and willing to be healed."

"The problem," he continued, "is that too many people are using the herb without proper instruction, without proper invocation. They turn to the plant, or others like it, for lack of an identity, and they give up their will, expecting the plant to perform some miraculous wonder within, instead of considering a symbiotic relationship with the plant, by which they can retain their souls. But they are weak, and they give up their souls, turning into mindless zombies who lie to themselves and everybody else, opening the gate for impostor spirits to enter and possess them."

Amdusias couldn't agree more, and this was exactly why he was so concerned about the prolific spread of the plant in the land, numbing the minds of so many who don't understand what it is or how to properly use it. They smoke the herb while they drink or smoke other intoxicants, or they smoke without real purpose, and it takes over their lazy lives.

"But if Buer already understands these risks, then why does he promote and package it for gain?" mused Amdusias.

"You see," continued Buer, as if reading the mind of Amdusias, "the truth is that I am split-minded and possessed myself...."

He paused and saw that Amdusias and Malthus were listening, so he continued his confession. "It began many years ago when I fell from grace, because I failed in my duties and made a terrible choice which led to the failing health and unhappiness of a very dear loved one...."

"Ah, the painful realization of free will," responded Amdusias.

"Yes, it was," Buer confirmed, then continued. "So, I set about to find a cure for this disease, and it led me down a very strange and winding road where I found the secrets of health, but also the dynamics of rage and pestilence."

"Rage and pestilence?" asked Amdusias, leading him along.

"Yes, the doorway by which the demons of guilt and fear enter our thoughts, split our minds, and lead us to commit insane and criminal acts."

"So, you went down this path yourself?"

"Yes, I did. I made terrible mistakes. I was driven by fear and allowed diverse influences to take over and control my mind, while I became a mere spectator in my own life."

Amdusias wondered if he had rehearsed this speech beforehand. Perhaps Buer felt he needed to be upright and honest about his failures of the past and the real potential for abuse of the Bhang, to clear his conscience and help his clients? Was this enough? Wasn't he still contributing to the corruption of society?

"The man I have become today is still an empty shell compared to my original propitious nature," he said with a mix of humility and pride. "I have much more to do in this life. Much more to prove to myself and others. I feel comfortable, stable with my outer structure, but vacant inside...."

He picked up a tied sack of Bhang from the table, looked at it, then tossed it back on the table.

"I used to fill my soul with this, but then I realized it was just an illusion... just a substitute for the real thing. So, I quit."

Amdusias was fascinated with this speech and wondered where it was going, still listening intently. "It sounds like you were questioning your purpose in life, perhaps feeling unfulfilled?" he asked honestly.

"I felt like an empty vessel on the potter's lathe, spinning around like the Earth, so fertile and full of life to give, but overflowing with agitation and rage!"

"Enraged about what?" asked Amdusias, very curious now.

"Enraged in my mind, enraged with myself, enraged with the Spirit which filled, or failed to fill my hollow soul. I felt the capacity to grow and flourish, but I was stuck in this cycle, subject to the whims of the heavens."

"Ah. You felt the heavens were not utilizing your potential?"

"Well, that's just it. It wasn't the heavens, it was me. I was a weak vessel who allowed my shape and contents to be changed all the time by whoever wanted to make use of it. My mind kept changing, changing, changing... all the time."

Amdusias was developing a profound respect for this man Buer. He certainly had a way with words.

"I learned about this idea of eternal bliss and wanted a shortcut," continued Buer. "But... eventually it all came crashing down, and I was no closer to enlightenment than I was when I started, and really the best path for me was to delay gratification and focus on temporal and worldly pursuits for a time."

"Temporal and worldly pursuits?" Amdusias wondered to himself if this was where he would start justifying his business.

"Yes, because it was all I really knew. I could pretend that I was enlightened or somehow connected to some higher intelligence, but what about my own mind? What did I know about myself? I wanted to reconnect with the Earth and really understand my own powers and my callings, and how they relate. You know, am I shrinking or growing? Coming or going? Do I have any real control, or am I being controlled? Am I setting goals and achieving my desires or not?"

It all sounded good, thought Amdusias, but it was just rhetoric. Where was this all really going?

"These little accomplishments really matter, you see, and I realized they are the foundation of all the 'supernatural' abilities. It starts with realizing that I am not just the empty vessel, but rather I am the Watcher of myself. I can understand and become involved with myself by contemplating *myself* and recognizing that *I* am One with the Divine Self which abides in all things."

"Hmm," offered Amdusias, and Malthus nodded knowingly. "Sounds true enough."

"For me, the solution began with recognizing the rage inside, realizing that it boiled down to simple feelings of unsatisfied fertility inside."

"You mean sexuality?" asked Amdusias bluntly.

"That was a part of it, yes... and it seems to be a big part for many people. Some of us confuse our procreative urge and become totally obsessed, as if it is all that matters in the world, and we let it rule our minds. We stop using our higher abilities and functions, because we think sexuality is the only means of showing and receiving affection. And it becomes a centerpiece of our existence and purpose."

Buer suddenly felt self-conscious about his speech. "I'm sorry for rambling. The truth is that if people really understood what I'm trying to say here, then I might go out of business because people would realize they don't need this silly herb either."

"Don't apologize," responded Amdusias quickly. "Truthfully, I've noticed this is a big problem in our lands."

"Yes, and this is why I insist on having this conversation with my big customers," Buer continued, "because I want to raise awareness and challenge us to take responsibility, restraining ourselves from allowing unnecessary modifications of the mind."

Amdusias thought back to some lessons he had learned about meditation and concentration with his mind. "So, you're saying we can do this – control the mind – through contemplation, starting with an awareness of our feelings and nature around us."

"Yes, through contemplation of nature, exactly... her balance, activities, and inertias. There is ONE earth," he emphasized, "just as there is only one Heaven. One body, and one Spirit. The ear connects us to the ether, and the bright light in the soul, the intellect, relates to the Divine Self, and so, all of this allows us to attain knowledge by degrees, exactly when we need it."

"The body and mind produce all the love and healing we need, just as the Earth and the Lord provide for all their children," added Malthus-Agla.

"Yes!" exclaimed Buer. "This Bhang is a product of the Earth, but we must remember the whole. There are some who will benefit from this medicine, but many more will suffer and abuse the same because they have an incorrect understanding of themselves and the Earth....

"Let us remember the Earth, how she manifests herself, sometimes mildly and other times with firmness. She supports and contains all of us with unlimited capacity, waits patiently on the direction of the Lord, and advocates for her children with perfect comprehension and astounding brightness."

"Her manifestations are diverse, from the frost signaling the onset of winter to the magnificence of man-made temples!"

He picked up the sack again, then continued. "Earth is docile like this sack, tied up and completely subservient to the Master, never seeking praise, simply existing like an outer garment with a singular purpose. But the Earth is not an inanimate garment, but rather a dynamic formation whose dragons rise up in the fields to fight and spill blood to fertilize her fields, regenerating new crops and filling the air with the essence of life!"

He was waving his hands around for emphasis, then stopped to compose himself and catch his breath. The others nodded and took a breath as well, as the discussion had taken a turn into a profoundly deep subject, and it was a lot to take in all at once.

After a pause, Amdusias broke the silence with a serious tone. "Buer, let's say I take your advice and refrain from purchasing any Bhang. What's next? What if I told you I was looking for an excuse to cut off the supply of Bhang, and your sermon here was exactly what I needed to hear, to fully convince me. What you're saying here sounds extremely important, like maybe we need to take action to put an end to the trade and find something new."

"It makes no difference to me, my friends. I speak openly and honestly to ensure customers are fully informed to the best of my ability and conscience, but the business will continue to thrive because there are many legitimate uses of the Bhang, not only in the medical field but also in the industrial. We have clients in diverse fields, and thousands of workers to support in addition. My clients are all legitimate, but... there is another king whose dealings and intentions are not so noble as mine."

Amdusias raised his eyebrows, worried that his cover was blown but still trying to save face. Was Buer's entire speech just a ruse to trick them?

Meanwhile Malthus-Agla seemed unaffected, as if he knew Buer's intentions all along. He asked bluntly, "Will you lead us to this other king?"

"No," said Buer. "It's not my business. But I can do one better for you. I want you to meet a stranger."

They went back out the gates and joined with the crew members, who were patiently biding their time, carving wood and making conversation with each other and the outer perimeter guards. Orobas was glad to see they made it back without any issues.

"Saddle up, my friends, we're going further south, southwest," said Buer with a flare.

They traveled for about two hours on horseback and arrived in a small homestead just before nightfall.

The homestead was bustling with energy, with folks excitedly walking to and fro as live music emanated from a nearby bar.

Buer pointed up to the marquee over a prominent building, which was lit up with lights and hosting a main attraction.

People poured into the building, and tickets were being sold on the street corners by auctioneers.

"Remember what I said about dragons fighting?" asked Buer. He pointed up to a poster advertising the main event of the night, featuring two dragon-like opponents in a grudge match.

He'd kept Amdusias and the others in suspense about the purpose of their journey thus far, and Amdusias was uneasy, as if they were being led into a trap.

"What's this about?" asked Orobas.

"Just entertainment, my friends," answered Buer, "and we'll meet one of them after the fight." He gestured to the opponent on the left side of the poster, with his name in bold letters: *Hauresh*, who appeared like a leopard with dragon wings.

They took their places and watched eagerly as the match began, as fans cheered and jeered with a rumble that filled the stadium, and an announcer's voice murmured over a loudspeaker with unintelligible comments. They were close enough to see the fighters clearly as they emerged, and the rumble in the stadium grew louder and more excited.

Amdusias was struck by the flaming fire in the eyes of Hauresh[3]. His expression conveyed raw determination and fearlessness.

The fighters were both bred for strength and skills in the arena, but the opponent was no match for Hauresh. He won the match handily and left his opponent bleeding profusely from multiple cuts and lacerations, unable to see through his blackened eyes which were swollen shut.

Hauresh had little more than a scratch on his body as he held up his wobbly opponent for a final blow, and the audience cried out with an unquenchable bloodlust, *"Finish him! Finish him!!!...,"* but when his opponent cried for mercy, Hauresh let his opponent fall to the mat and walked back toward his corner.

The announcer's murmur came over the cackling loudspeaker to declare the victor, as the audience exploded with cheering.

Several fights broke out in the stands between fans, and security personnel tried to break them up.

Amid the drone of the crowd, Buer motioned to Amdusias and Malthus-Agla, who were both not particularly amused with the fighting event. The match was uneven and extremely brutal. But they followed Buer through the hoard and made their way back to a staging area behind the scenes, where the din of the arena was somewhat muted, and they could talk again.

Buer exchanged a bag of Bhang with one of the guards for access to a private area, obviously not the first time he had been this way before.

And then, he led them back around into a more secluded area where they passed by another guard who nodded once at them, then through a doorway into Huaresh's private area.

"As fearsome as ever, my friend!" Buer called out to Hauresh.

Hauresh grunted and seemed annoyed with the immediate visit after his fight, but apparently had fond feelings for Buer and let it pass. "Buer. What brings you here, old friend?"

"Let's discuss elsewhere, friend," replied Buer. "I've reserved some space at the local lodge where we plan to stay tonight. Let's make our way over there, and we'll eat like royalty to celebrate and discuss."

Hauresh scanned the strangers with his fiery eyes, striking fear into Amdusias before he looked away.

"All right Buer. Let's catch up."

Over their meal, the conversation took an interesting turn when Buer asked how Hauresh was coming along with his latest book.

And as they came to find out, Hauresh was not only a powerful fighter in the ring, but also a distinguished author and scholar who governed a nearby university, the University of St. Mihyael, where their research specialized in many subjects, including the cures for disease and infections.

Amdusias was astonished at the diverse talents of this stranger in a strange land, and suddenly realized there was far more to this trip than mere amusement.

Hauresh described with pleasure his recent trip to the hospital, where he was able to meet with a patient undergoing treatments and offer a blessing. The patient was completely cured of all pain and infection, needing no medicine to restore his health, crediting Hauresh for healing him.

"He was in perfect spirits," Hauresh described with some pride, "and he told me he hadn't felt so good in years as he walked out. It was a special case because the cure was inside him all along, and the therapy was based on guided imagery to help him get into communication with energy centers *in his body*, to activate and manufacture the cure *within his own body*. All I had to do was remind him who he was; what his *body* was already doing."

Malthus-Agla nodded as if he was familiar with the process.

"The irony here is that I am suffering, and I cannot find any peace in this place. This was supposed to be my resting place, but I feel tortured and tired, stuck in this... place... with so much energy and so many tools to do such wonderful things, but also somehow trapped and limited. I still feel like a stranger, uncomfortable and restless."

He paused in thought, then continued, "One of my professors said something the other day which left a distinct impression. He said, '*It is only necessary to go, not necessarily to live.*' Have you heard that expression before?"

The others shook their heads, and he continued, "So, I've been thinking about it, and I realized I'm not living up to my potential. I want to banish mischief within the gates of industry and aid the education of the poor. I'm tired of the drink and all the revelry, tired of ignoring my intuition which tells me to be upright and sober in my habits. I crave larger intellect and superior wisdom which the Spirit alone can teach, and I feel a duty within the dictates of my conscience to strive for nobility and balance."

Amdusias was awestruck by his eloquence, and nodded his head in agreement, stopping once to shake his head in disbelief about the strange sequence of events. Could this Hauresh be the key to restoring order and balance in the kingdom? He looked over at Buer with a questioning look, and Buer smiled back.

Buer took the opportunity to suggest what was on their minds. "Hauresh, how about you take a trip to the northern kingdom of Aychael with my friends here? They have some troubles with order and a lack of integrity in the society, and they could use a strong influence like yours to help. You might learn a thing or two as well in the process."

Hauresh hardly even needed the suggestion. He was ready to leave the nest and wander into new territory. He wanted to start fresh in a new environment. So, he accepted the proposal and thanked the travelers for their hospitality and their willingness to accept his companionship on the return trip.

"May the Great Master of our Universe give us the strength and wisdom to faithfully perform our duties!" announced Hauresh.

As they loaded their wagons, Amdusias contemplated the Earth with her valuable passengers, spinning with constant mystery, offering herself to all who would take hold and join the journey. He looked down at the soil and saw a small sprout emerging its tiny branches, destined to create another seed and start the process all over again.

He was so inspired by the sight that he spoke aloud, "May God bless the Earth, my friends. She is the mother of all, the finest of the linens, the richest of all the soils and all other formations, tacitly firm and unlimited in capacity as she rotates faithfully and perfectly in the heavens. She is the definition and the goal of all good fortune. *May God bless her!*"

The others smiled and nodded in agreement, and some echoed the final phrase as they set out upon their return journey.

[1] *Barbatos* is a great Duke who is normally invisible to man, but he appears once per year when the sun is in Sagittary, along with four noble kings and their hosts.

His true name is כהתאל (*Kehethael*), of the Order of Virtues, which order he never failed to respect even in his fallen state. He rules thirty legions of spirits, and despite his dark side he gives greater understanding among men, usually by means of subtle verbal communication (and in writing afterwards).

And by virtue of this verbalization with his voice, he can also reverse and reveal the secrets of spells laid by magicians, which may sometimes open vaults filled with hidden treasures.

Part of his gift is understanding the voices of others, including the singing of birds or the barking of dogs. And then he uses that understanding to reconcile friends and mend governments.

But his fall came after he misused this greater understanding. His pride became blasphemy, and crops withered in his presence. He lost his sensitivity for crops due to his love for the animals, which is ironic considering his love for working with agriculture in the countryside, and his governance of agricultural production. He forgot and neglected his relationship with God and Earth.

So, he temporarily failed in his humility, but ultimately, he rises toward God by kneeling in sincere prayer and petition, by which he drives off evil spirits by seeking and understanding the light.

An important distinction recognized by Barbatos is that which exists between sentiments and principles, and he is known to use words sparingly and follow through on obligations. It's not that he avoids words; quite the contrary (as suggested above), he is interested in well-placed words to increase understanding and motivate positive action. But he places his passions in check, and he can easily see the hypocrisy in others who like to talk big but fall short in practice. He has taken his calling very seriously, as he is the final focal point of all the formations.

He feels some trepidation, yet an overriding sense of calm, reassured by his own commitment to integrity and honesty.

He is sure-footed, well-founded, secure, immovable, immutable, and grounded in the most literal sense imaginable. His wits and nerves cannot be shaken more than he can bear, because he knows his master and maker, and he stays close to the Lord in reverent kneeling and supplication. (Reference *Psalms 95:6*)

He has no pride other than pride in our maker, and he is happy to sound off with joyful noise with psalms, praising the one who mastered the depths and heights of the earth, the seas and dry lands that he made.

He remembers well the hard-heartedness of those who wandered in the wilderness for forty years and never entered into his rest.

[2] The first child of Barbatos is known as *Buer*, the great president who carries on in the strength of his father and mother.

Like his father, Buer also makes his physical manifestation or appearance in the fall when the sun is in Sagittarius, yet he always exists and speaks subtly as his father before him.

He speaks of philosophical, scientific, and logical artistry, especially as pertains to the herbs and plants and their virtues. With his words and through his herbology, he heals distempers in men and gives good familiars, starting with his fifty legions of fine spirits. His eternal name is אלדיה (*Aladiah*) the Propitious.

Aladiah fell temporarily from grace and became Buer when he failed in his duties, making a choice which led to failing health of a loved one. And as a result of this tragedy, he felt a growing fear and uncertainty, and he longed for something to fill the void within his soul. His body itched with agitation and rage, and he lost his balance.

But over time, he found redemption and progression toward eternal life, due to his conscientious choices in life's crossroads, choosing the right path with guidance and inspiration from the Supreme Being. He began to see himself as a sprouting idea, pushing beyond the threshold of the seed, wending his way, sprouting branches, leaves, buds, flowers, and fruit.

And as a result, he came to govern the cure of disease by ruling the dynamics of rage and pestilence.

Thereby he enjoys and shares good health and success in all his undertakings. He is particularly helpful to those who are now wrestling with the demons of guilt, fear, and a criminal past; those who have a desire to make amends and seek resolution.

He helps us to realize our own fertility and encourages us to be passive and detached, and yet disciplined with mindfulness.

[3] The most successful and beautiful dragon is known as האוראש (*Hauresh*, sometimes called *Flaurob*), the great Duke, a mighty leopard with wings whose eyes are flaming with fire and whose visage strikes fear into all except those who understand him.

Thirty-six legions of spirits follow him and take pleasure in carrying out his works, including dark works of guile and deceit, destroying and burning any who stand against their master. Hauresh is very loyal to his own master and possessive as well, and he drives off any spirits who tempt or try to control him.

Hauresh is none other than the mighty and well-known spirit מהיאל (*Mihyael*, or *Michael*), the one who gave life to all things, the original "Alli" who rose to new heights never reached before, then fell dramatically to serve as the first and archetypal human being named *ADAM*, the primordial man.

He originally rose to fame and glory for defeating the great red dragon with seven heads, the one known as the Devil or Satan, casting him out of heaven to the earth with all his dark angels. And yet Michael also fell to the earth himself, some would say on purpose, perhaps because was tired of having no opposition, perhaps because he could no longer bear to look down upon the scattered strength of the Earth, saying, *"The Mare is so strong, but whom shall be delivered?"*

His allegiance was to the Father, whose eye looks down upon all who fear him or hope in his mercy.

And therefore, his is the story of a boy who rebelled against the docile mother to stand up for the father. He was angry with the complacency of the former, so he developed pride and ego by distinguishing himself from Purusha (the Universal Principle). So, ironically, in his effort to destroy evil, he fell and joined the fallen world himself. And he was bipolar, just like his mother, the Earth, yet enraged with the pride and fighting spirit of Mars, so he waged war against himself in the process.

Adam was the epitome of righteous adoration of the Father because he sought constantly for counsel with fear and hope. But his faith failed, and he sinned against the father's will by partaking of the forbidden fruit, after which he immediately felt the influence of his great mistake, and he sought to repent with newfound knowledge between good and evil, somehow endowed with a gift of wisdom as a result of his rebellion.

And after being cast out of the garden, Adam was a stranger in a strange land with keen awareness of the severity of his situation, sensing the immediate need to move ahead, in the correct course.

He had heard much about being firm and correct from the angels, who prepared him for probation, but after the Fall, he had a real sense of the grand importance of life, so he humbled himself in dutiful service and reverent worship.

He was terrified at first, but in worshipping God he found security and felt well-grounded in the territory. And at times it all seemed very familiar, so he wondered if he had been to the Earth before, and he suspended his judgment, feeling quiet rest within and a bright fire without.

There is more to the story of Michael-Adam-Hauresh that is not recorded in the book of *Genesis*:

At first, having partaken of the fruit and fallen from the grace and immediate presence of God, he saw himself as a mean soul, whose character was extremely low and pathetic compared to the grandeur of God or the world, so he subjected himself to take on any and all burdens, and setting himself up for further failure, because he thought he deserved the punishment and suffering. So, he brought calamity on himself, his family, and all near him.

After some time, he found that despite his foolish intentions to sabotage himself, there were many good creations (other people) who sought to help him. He realized that these others were also suffering at times, and they could help each other, so they began to flourish together, and he took up residence in a lodge built by such trusted friends.

He had no complaints for a time.

But a certain rage and anxiety began to grow deeply inside him, and he burned the lodging house in a fit of desperation, seeking to re-establish communication with God, believing that God might accept the lodge as a burnt offering. Many of his friends perished in the fire, and he was left alone once again, feeling like a guilty misfit on the Earth, forced to deal with his insanity and the peril of lost dear relationships.

The only injuries he sustained were cuts, burns, and scratches, but one lesion became permanent as a reminder of the pain, continually breaking open after only partially healing.

So, he was mentally torn because of the awkward juxtaposition of his condition. He had the means to be great and the tools to be productive and creative, yet he trudged through his days with terrible anxiety and depression as he waited in his resting place, hoping for better days and forcing himself to work.

But he remembered overcoming difficult challenges in the past, and with some help, he emerged successfully from this drought by taking steps in order, with a continual flow of consciousness. His mind returned to the Earth, and he prayed that his self-will would be swallowed up and atoned for gracefully in time.

Hauresh wanted to take part in the great plan of God the Creator, so he cried out and purified himself, and he felt the Spirit again.

In time, he even learned to smile again as he felt the love of God, the gentleness and kindness and mercy of the Creator, who still remembered him as a child and wanted him to be happy.

So, he left his resting place and became engaged, and he took a risk by hunting after a pheasant.

He shot his first arrow and missed, but hit successfully with the second attempt, which brought new purpose and high praise among his people. A glow of elegant brightness surrounded him, and he was able to see his blunders as a learning experience.

And over the years, the details of his great mistakes slipped into amnesia, but one day while breathing in the air, he noticed a bird was burning its nest, and all the memories returned in a torrent. At first, he laughed at the irony, but then he cried out in empathy as all the pain returned, and he witnessed the plight of the bird. So, he re-committed to connect with God in repentance again.

"Am I still a stranger?" he asked.

And he committed to lose himself in the greater effort of God.

Hauresh became highly distinguished in literature, and now he governs the wise orators, servants, and professors of the world, protecting them against adversities, disease, and the infectious attacks from wild beasts.

Chapter 10 – Kingdom

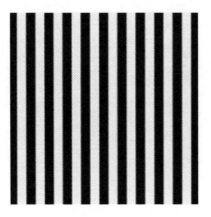

Foreword

The spirit of the Earth, the endpoint of all Yetsiratic formation, puts on her luminous garments and operates with intelligence, having taken a form, but not in the materialistic physical sense (heavy and corporeal). She consists of pure and refined matter, yet the forms may still change, and it interacts with the material plane as we measure and experience it.

So, we enter the latter domain in which physical actions occur, where spirits may dawn "shells" upon their luminous garments, and the Queen of the Qliphoth, the Cherubim, and the Shekinah rule the Matrix as bride of Microprosopus, which is the lesser countenance of the earth, in which Barbatos-Kehethael dwells.

The subject of Malkuth is wonderfully diverse and yet so simple. Consider botanical life, plants, trees, shrubs, flowers, and weeds, and their counterparts in nature, the insects and animals who serve as her messengers and movers. This is an all-in-one package of splendid proportions, which is not typified by any elemental trigrammatic emblem or spirit.

It is personified in the spirit Ashtaroth-Reyeyael and her companion Gamori-Povyael, whom we will meet in this chapter.

The ultimate spring of life is God's well of eternal living water, which is referenced by the Biblical prophets such as Isaiah, Jeremiah, Zechariah, and Jesus Christ. This water is available to all who will submit and choose to draft and drink from this unchanging source, a central well whose fashion never changes. The water comforts saints and sinners alike, and it stimulates us to mutual helpfulness. The going feels slow and painful amidst surrounding peril, but with measured steps, plans, and dexterity to follow, nourishment and fortune will result.

We turn to אדני (Adonai) in reverent reflection to consider the Kingdom, and we ask how we may contribute to the Kingdom. We do so in small, repetitive, cumulative ways, through the standard toil of daily labors or more intellectual pursuits with synergy, conversation, and uplifting dialogue – open, powerful, humble, relaxed, and good humored, neither proud nor haughty. We may be "nose breathers" but we find great strength and security in Adonai, the teacher and great merciful master.

Being the seedless one, and nameless except through reflection, the Queen Matrona accepts that her needs are secondary to the needs of her husband, the Microprosopus, and that the timeline is his, not hers. Is there anything she can do to accelerate the process to encourage him to grace her with his presence?

She feels grateful that he is still communicative, even if only to summarily dismiss her and to tell her to be patient. But she fears he may make her wait a long time or even forever.

She expresses herself and reflects what she observes, magnifying both the good and the bad to accelerate the inevitable.

(Please note, this is not to suggest male dominion over females, but rather specifically refers to the unique dynamic between Queen Matrona and Microprosopus, and the tables will turn.)

She wonders if she is the only one. Can he really be trusted?

She retains her faith in him, realizing that he is mostly honest even if he gets carried away in fantasy, which serves a purpose. And she gets back to basics and core competencies, focusing on principal duties and feeling good about confronting her thoughts and expressing herself.

She feels the glory of the divine presence within, as bright light in a deep, restful dwelling place, very feminine by its definition. She recognizes that she has great value indeed, and she feels good about her ability to serve, like a child or cherub.

Her specialty is to break up the foundation of the complex nature of all matter and return to pure elemental richness. She does so with just an innocent smile or a simple laugh, resenting nothing, judging nobody, putting all things into perspective with childlike hope and courage (heart). There is a certain chubbiness to her, along with a profound respect for free will, which is her saving grace and part of her appeal.

Back in the land of Mahashiah, Andras

finally replied to Amdusias's letter.

In his response, he asked Amdusias for a meeting in the place where they had met before, in the mountainous valley between Mahashiah and Samigina, where Andras was anointed king in the land before they separated.

Andras was skeptical about the meeting, but he had some hope that perhaps they could reconcile their differences.

And when Amdusias arrived in Samigina with Orobas, Malthus-Agla, and Hauresh, he read the letter and quickly consulted the Lord on the matter, desperately wanting to resolve the corruption in his lands, which had grown even worse while they were away. The people were vile and hateful toward each other, productivity was down, and they had lost the essence of worship. They clung to their own strength and wisdom, and they measured themselves by the strength of their military might, ruling by intimidation.

Bune and Orias were uneasy with each other, and they took turns speaking negatively about each other to Amdusias, but Orias had the upper hand. He held a stronghold of control over Bune and all the rest by tricking them to commit crimes, then holding the crime over them as leverage to manipulate their souls.

Bune wanted to escape the tyranny, but he was torn and tried to maintain allegiance, because he was also guilty by association. He had his own guilty lies to protect. And they operated in the shadows and somehow kept an outward appearance of strength, yet they suffered great instability inside.

Amdusias presided over many cities in the land, and despite the circumstances, he still had a special affinity for Samigina and its two leaders, Orias and Bune. They had sacrificed much to build a mighty civilization and seaport town, and he felt its shipping industry was the only hope they had to successfully cross the Great Waters with a migration into the new promised land.

So, he went to the Lord in prayer to express his concerns, asking for guidance to save the civilization and carry on in his mission.

The answer from the Lord was unclear to Amdusias because his mind was not clear enough to receive the answer.

So, he prayed again, and again.

He even asked his counselors to pray on his behalf and communicate their responses.

They received no answer for many days, but finally one of his priests purified himself and made humble offerings to the Lord, praying without ceasing for a full day and a night to inquire about the will of the Lord.

And the answer finally came that Amdusias would have to make a choice to serve the Lord and leave behind the corruption if he wanted to save himself and his people. The choice seemed clear, yet the Lord warned him to be watchful and careful, because one mistake may cloud his mind and cause the entire plan to fail.

Amdusias considered the stories of old in which the kings and prophets were given a similar ultimatum.

Some chose to follow the Lord without reservation, and they were blessed for obedience and worship, while others chose the arm of flesh, lost the blessings of the Lord, and suffered defeat. He had experienced the same pattern in his own life.

He was disappointed because the Lord did not hear his prayers, or rather because he felt unworthy to receive the response from the Lord, so he resolved to purify himself.

"Obedience to the Lord is a delicate balance," Amdusias offered to his companions, "for on the one hand, we feel commanded to prove ourselves with righteous dominion and total control over our minds and bodies, but on the other hand, we must submit to his will and recognize our weakness and complete dependence. Too often, I have attempted to prove my strength through force and self-will, and I forgot whose battle this is. And that's the balancing act, we must remember that *this is the Lord's battle*, and the most important goal is to seek His will and his blessing, then put all our faith and trust in Him. *Only within the bounds that the Lord has set, we exercise our self-will and control.*"

Amdusias travelled northeasterly with Orobas, Malthus-Agla, Hauresh, and eight others, to the land designated by Andras, where they finally met with Andras and his companions: Andrealphus, Glasya-Labolas, Belial and twelve others.

Andras and his companions had pitched a small camp near a brook, hidden among the trees.

A band of spies and warriors had been sent by Orias and Bune, and they were hiding now, monitoring Amdusias and his group.

And furthermore, Buer had also sent a network of spies to watch over the situation, with principal orders to ensure the safety of Barbatos and Hauresh. Buer was a little suspicious of Amdusias, but overall, he trusted and appreciated his intentions, so he also ordered his spies to watch out for Amdusias and Malthus-Agla, and report back with any news of importance.

Finally, there was yet another intelligence network, which was the most technologically advanced, leveraging new technology learned from the Haziaelians, by which Andras and his group could send and receive messages with an operator in Xabuviah, who could then communicate with the air forces of Zagan and the armies of Kimaris in Afrika, who stood by to help.

The messages could be sent instantly over long distances.

Furthermore, the winged lions of Napula and other-dimensional fighters of Volak patrolled the skies from both sides of the veil to support the cause of Andras, needing no artificial technology to stay in constant observance and instant communication.

The encounter between the two groups was tense at first.
Several of them were ready to fight, with their weapons drawn.
But Andras and Amdusias quickly calmed the others with their smiles and a handshake, which became an embrace.

Most stood by still and quietly, but some fidgeted nervously as they waited expectantly for the two to begin talking.

"It's been a very long time, my friend, too long," said Amdusias. "Much has changed."

"Yes, it has," Andras affirmed with a nod.

Amdusias leaned in for one more embrace, and whispered softly, "We're being watched. Let us proceed with caution."

Then he raised his voice, pandering to spies of Orias and Bune, and said, "I hope you will visit the sea-port town of Samigina and meet some key figures there. You'll be amazed what we have accomplished. I know our past encounters ended poorly, but I believe we can find some common ground and help our respective lands to prosper, trading goods and knowledge."

Andras nodded again and spoke, "This sounds like...."

"*Aaaaaahhhh!*" came a blood-curdling yelp from the distance, interrupting their conversation and causing a panic all around.

They circled their heads with weapons drawn, totally confused. "It's a trap!" yelled Glasya-Labolas, and they heard more rustling in the trees, more fighting and yelling.

Suddenly a pair of Haaiahan dragons buzzed in from behind Amdusias' party and landed, holding a struggling captive between them – one of Buer's spies.

Hauresh was startled, and his eyes glowed with an angry flame.

"You were being followed by spies, my Lord," the lead dragon uttered to Amdusias, "What shall...."

Hauresh exploded with fury. He attacked both dragons himself, knocking one to the side and disabling the other easily, ready to continue his assault.

The crowd scattered and brave fighters stepped up to contend.

"Wait!" yelled Amdusias, stepping up in between Hauresh and the dragons. "This is a misunderstanding! Let us collect ourselves and discuss like rational beings!"

Hauresh listened and stopped, but it was too late to stop the escalating fights in the distant trees, as Haaiahans skirmished with the weaker Aladiahans, capturing and carrying them upward into the skies, presumably back to Samigina for questioning and trials.

Amid all the confusion and fighting, Amdusias spoke loudly, "These are not our emissaries, but rather just fools quick to spy and make assumptions. Please let us trust in each other and return to Samigina to clear this mess and resume our discussion."

With some reluctance and confusion, the parties agreed and made their way.

Following the advice of Belial, Andras found a private moment to send a message, to request support from the armies of Zagan and Kimaris, and he prayed silently for a safe delivery.

Orias seethed with anger as he accused Amdusias. "You expect us to uphold security in the land, but then you wander off for a secret meeting with our past sworn enemies, expecting nothing will happen?"

Amdusias ignored his venomous words and asked, "What about the Aladiahan spies? How will they be handled?"

"Buer has already negotiated for their release. He claims that he had no knowledge of their mission to spy on us, but he agreed to offer a substantial amount of Bhang and other goods in exchange for his men. He will try them in their own courts."

Amdusias nodded. "Any fatalities?"

"Two," answered Bune. "One of my own, one Aladiahan."

Amdusias let out an audible sigh of disappointment.

Then Orias stated in a deceptively calm voice, "Please answer some questions of my own, Amdusias. What was the purpose of your secret rendezvous? What shall we do with your guests in our holding area...?"

"One of whom assaulted and injured my men," interjected Bune.

"Let me handle it," offered Amdusias bluntly, ignoring the question about the rendezvous. "Suffice it to say that these visitors will not be staying very long, and we may be able to set up some sort of mutually beneficial trade agreement with them. I didn't think it was necessary to involve everybody in this...."

Orias breathed in, then exhaled audibly to express his frustration, and his snakes slithered with an unusual anxiety. He looked left, then right, then up at the sky to observe the sun and the planets, then down at his ring, fashioned by dwarf inventors, then pulled out his glowing pad to take a note. Finally, looking at Amdusias, he said, "I apologize for intruding on your privacy, Amdusias, and I will withdraw my men from the current surveillance detail. I'm interested to know how your conversation goes."

Amdusias looked at Bune, who nodded all three heads and lowered his spear in deference, and the three leaders departed with the pretense of an agreement.

A riot had erupted in the holding area.

Warriors were fighting fiercely with the Haaiahan dragons, and even Glasya-Labolas and Hauresh joined the skirmish. They had nearly overpowered them when Amdusias and Bune showed up on the scene to break it up.

"What's going on in there?!" demanded the voice of a Herahaelian officer, crackling over the intercom.

"Nothing, we're fine," lied Bune, who wrestled his dragons back while Amdusias calmed the others. "Let's pack it up, everybody. You're free to roam but please stay with your group and attend to your business. Please avoid unnecessary scuffles."

Amdusias motioned to follow him.

Before they left, Bune threatened candidly in a low quiet voice, "Surely you realize that we aren't going to let this go so easily. You'd better watch yourselves."

Amdusias scuttled around his chambers nervously, which caused some anxiety in the overpacked room. Orobas and some of the others waited outside on watch, but in attendance were Andras, Amdusias, Andrealphus, Glasya-Labolas, Belial, Malthus-Agla, and Hauresh.

Amdusias turned on some sort of security device at the door, then breathed to collect himself before turning to the group.

"Some of you already know that my intention is to traverse the Great Waters to the new promised land, as directed by the Lord," he started.

There were nods in the room, as most of them had heard directly or through rumors about the planned mission, vaguely proposed by Amdusias in his letter to Andras.

Amdusias continued, "We need to take a ship from the harbor, and do so quickly in the night, tonight."

"Tonight?" echoed several in the room.

"How will we pull off such a timeline?"

"Waiting any longer will only add complications," he continued. "The Lord has not spoken to me directly in recent times, but of this mission I am sure, and I am also sure that we have the right group for the job. We must leave Samigina behind to be directed by Orias and Bune, and they will not accompany us."

"Are you joking?" asked Belial incredulously. "What's to prevent them from following us and destroying our ship?"

"This is the least of our problems," offered Amdusias sheepishly. "Phenex of Aniael reported to me that the waters are treacherous, and a strange island with terrible creatures lies in their midst. We must put our faith in the Lord and pray to Him to deliver this mission successfully for us. It is not up to any one of us to win this battle, but rather to let the Lord deliver it."

The room was silent, but most agreed with his statement.

So, Amdusias provided a specific location to meet at midnight, at the harbor on one of the ships, which was ready for departure. Nightfall had almost arrived, so there wasn't much time left. They broke up their meeting to make preparations.

"Rrrrrrrreeeeeeeeeeeeeeeemm, rrrreeeeeeeeeeeeeemmmmm...."

A loud siren filled the night air, causing soldiers and citizenry to panic and run around in the streets, some to take cover and some to assume battle stations.

Thousands of invaders came droning in from the southeastern skies while the Haaiahan dragons and other fighting units tried to prepare their defenses. Omabaelian bulls and armored skycrafts, descending with hordes of mounted Manaqueliahan warriors, had arrived in force, led by Zagan and Kimaris respectively.

Then a blinding light, brighter than the noonday sun, lit up the entire landscape for a long second, causing fear to overcome all the soldiers of Samigina.

Haaiahan dragons fell from the sky, disoriented and disabled by the light, and Herahaelians were paralyzed and dumbfounded by the onslaught.

It was the light of Amon and his legions of angelic warriors, which approached with their swords drawn, ready to fight.

Those of Samigina had no choice but to surrender.

Andras's heart swelled with gratitude, with no doubt that Volak was leading an onslaught from the other side of the veil as well. He fell to his knees and closed his eyes to offer thanks to God above for delivering them.

Thus, it is said to this day,

"No armies in the world can stand up to the armies of Agares and Amon, who bring victory and glory."

Andras was bumped and aroused from prayer by Andrealphus, who smiled and said, "It's time to go! Let us offer thanks later."

The fellowship took the ship as was planned by Amdusias, and two more, with extra provisions and more confidence than ever.

They set out upon the water into new lands, with sure hope and faith that the Lord was directing their journey. They celebrated and offered sincere thanks, and they hoped to return to celebrate more with their allies on the mainland in the future.

Hovering over the ships in the sky was a single armored airship, piloted by Deanis, carrying a group of passengers and extra fuel.

"You know," said Amdusias with a smile as he looked back on the massive city, "I expect that Samigina will become greater than ever now, its mighty oak allowed to grow and to flourish, led by Orias and Bune, with new forces to bring balance."

He thought back to the time when he met Samigina of Ahlimiah, the great being who held a flashing hammer, and whose carriage was pulled by pair of goats, crackling and gnashing with sparks.

Samigina brought Orias into the world for a purpose, and he led him to Bune in the Haaiahan mountains. They had done much to move forward with the work of the Lord, he thought, and surely they would do much more in the future, having learned much.

"Look!"

It was Hauresh who first spotted the island off in the distance. He had been fixed upon the rolling horizon for days, ever since they departed from the port.

"What a beautiful island," he marveled.

Some of the others were not so optimistic or enchanted by the mysterious island, having heard stories of its horrors. But as they approached nearer, even the most skeptical couldn't ignore the surreal botanical life covering her rolling hills.

The island was lurid with vibrant color and stunning detail, bursting with energy through trees, shrubs, and flowers moving softly in the wind. The sunlight sparkled brightly against the crests of waves and created a spectacular contrast of colors with rich dark shadows across the landscape.

"Wow," uttered Hauresh again with reverence.

"We will pass this island to reach the new Promised Land," Amdusias announced with some hesitation.

"Then drop me off here," responded Hauresh. "I had a dream about this place, and I know I must explore her mysteries."

"Yeah, I want to explore as well!" said one of them.

Several others offered their support for Hauresh, but the majority wanted to play it safe and pass around the island.

An argument ensued, and they tried to settle the matter by casting lots, to determine the will of the Lord, but the cast only created additional debate, and they could not find an agreement.

Andras also consulted his necklace, but he received no response. So, he set aside the necklace and thought to ask his personal Urim and Thummim, the Lights and Perfection, which would give affirmative or negative answers when asked with sincerity.

He asked if they should send one of the ships to the island.

But the answer was unclear.

The only idea that seemed quite clear, upon which everybody including Hauresh could agree, was that they stood the best chance of survival it they stayed together as a group.

"If one ship sails off ahead, there's no telling if we'll ever meet up again," claimed Amdusias, which was answered by nods. They could stay in communication between ships for a while using special apparatuses, but the range was limited.

And while they discussed the matter, their discussion was interrupted by a panicked voice over the communication device.

"Something's coming... *ALERT*!" yelled Deanis, followed by some unintelligible noises.

They looked up and saw a massive flame-throwing dragon, approaching fast from the island, headed directly at the airship.

There was no time to think or react.

The dragon struck fiercely, latched its massive claws onto the hull of the airship, and turned to drag the craft back to the shore.

Andras could see a rider upon the dragon, holding a viper in its right hand, yelling noisome breathings, directing the capture.

And the ship hit the ground with a loud thud.

"We have no choice now," announced Amdusias. "The die has been cast. May God be with us as we rescue our compatriots."

The island was as lush up close as it was from a distance, but it was overshadowed with negativity and uncertainty now.

They were greeted by a swarm of dragonflies, which Belial called off with a wave of his hand. And they were motivated to move swiftly to find the craft and save their friends, so Hauresh led the way, hacking and using an uncanny ability with his eyes to burn away the brush as he pushed forward.

The island was full of insects and wild animals, prowling over the territory for survival, like machines with tasks to send messages and move things around.

"Who is controlling these things?" asked Andras to himself.

"There!" yelled Hauresh, completely unintimidated by whatever lay ahead. "There's the craft!"

The dragon hovered over the craft with its wings raised high, then hissed at the sight of the newcomers. Andras could see its nostrils flare and spew flame, followed by a stream of fire which blasted directly at them.

They instinctively held up their hands to hide their eyes from sure and sudden death.

But the flame never touched them, being split by some invisible force field in front of them, scorching the earth on either side. One unfortunate victim stood outside the protection of the field and was burned to a crisp.

"Did you do that?" Andrealphus asked Belial, who was glowing with a special aura surrounding his body.

Andras momentarily remembered the chariot of flame and the angels surrounding Belial, and he wondered what it meant.

"I don't know," he responded. "Not on purpose."

A feminine voice came thundering from beside the dragon, *"WHO DARES STEP FOOT ON MY SHORES?"*

And the angelic feminine creature approached, nearly naked and walking slowly with a viper in her right hand, standing erect.

"We do not fear your words, foul witch!" responded Hauresh with equal authority. "We have come for our lost compatriots, whom you snatched from the skies."

"They are dead," she responded coolly with a wide smile. "Anybody else care to cross me?"

Glasya-Labolas spread his wings and growled at the woman, ready to attack and flanked by his men, equally ready to attack. Hauresh and his men also assumed a battle stance, and Belial followed suit.

Andras felt intimidated, but he prepared for a fight, and he felt his blood surging to his eyes. "Just like old times," he thought.

The dragon was the first to strike, as the lady giggled alongside. It whipped its huge tail around and battered the entire group, then torched another victim, one of the Nith-Hayach. Then it stood up to its full height and wailed with a terrible noise as it breathed another streak of fire across the land, again scorching everything in its path.

Once again, the protective field of Belial saved the group, and Hauresh swung into action with a mighty slash to the beast's lower left leg, attempting to injure and knock him off balance.

Hauresh's wings were flared, and his leopard spots glowed with fire to match his eyes as he sliced through its flesh, and dragon blood sprayed from the wound.

But the beast was merely annoyed at the cut, and it stood up again to scream and breathe out another stream of fire.

"Throw me!" Andras yelled to Glasya-Labolas, as he saw an opportunity to attack and felt invincible for the moment.

Glasya-Labolas thought for a split second, then picked him up and hurled him like a javelin toward the massive beast.

Belial reacted quickly, distracting the beast in another direction, shielding himself from the flames while Andras landed on the head and violently gouged one of its eyes.

Blood sprayed everywhere as the beast violently shook its head and sent Andras hurtling to the side, tumbling to the ground, seriously injured.

The lady shrieked and uttered a curse from the side as Hauresh doubled in size, filled with rage. He scaled the dragon's back, gripped its head firmly with a choke hold, and then – the sound of tendons ripping apart filled the air as he tore the head from its body in a single upward twist, breaking its jaw and several other bones in the process.

Blood gushed from the head of the dragon, purple and yellow, and it flailed with one last struggle for survival, thrashing about to kill anything it could....

Then it fell loose and limp to the ground with a loud *thud*, shaking the earth and all who stood around.

The woman shrieked and began wailing uncontrollably.

"Who are you, woman?" bellowed Hauresh.

Andras regained his balance despite his right leg, badly injured. He scanned the area and saw more lifeforms in the distance, behind the damaged aircraft.

The woman buried her head in her arms and composed herself, then lifted her head again to speak. Her tone was solemn and shattered now, feeling defeated and ready to die.

"I am Ashtaroth of Reyeyael."

"What is your purpose on this island, Ashtaroth[1] of Reyeyael?" asked Hauresh, suddenly merciful, apparently enamored by her beauty and willing to give her a chance to live.

But she lashed out with a word at Hauresh, which stunned him just long enough for her to stage an attack.

Forty creatures emerged in a flash from the trees and barreled forward to protect their mistress, but they were repelled by the protective shield emanating around Belial, more powerful and expansive than ever.

Her face transformed into a nasty wraith with jaws wide open, and she pulled forward to bite Hauresh.

But he recovered and dodged the attack, and he slammed her to the ground, then finished her with a downward stroke of a sword, directly through her heart.

She shriveled and shrieked, then disappeared in a *poof* of smoke, leaving a trail of mist and dust.

And the sword clanged downward to the ground as Hauresh lost his balance and tumbled downward with a thud.

Everybody looked around in wonder, and nobody made a sound for a long second, as the wind began to churn around them.

And all the elements swirled around in a powerful vortex, converging to a single point between two massive pillars, gaining mass and velocity, and knocking men off their feet.

Many covered their eyes and fell to the ground as the storm flashed and rumbled in a torrent, and then all went silent again.

Ashtaroth had appeared again within the center, her body fully restored to its perfect state, standing amid her legion of forty.

"I AM that I AM," she uttered.

Then she snickered and looked at Hauresh with longing eyes. "You are a worthy fighter, leopard man. What is your name?"

"My name is Hauresh-Mihyael," he started. He wanted to talk but couldn't find the words. Had he met this woman before?

"Ah yes, Mihyael. You've come to rescue your sister, have you? But I have no need for you, Mihyael. I am self-sufficient now, as you can plainly see, for my legions are my seeds that issue forth from my five springs," she said cryptically with a smile, motioning behind her toward the center of the island.

She paused, and her face became deadly serious as she declared:

"I left you behind because this is the life I want. I am supported by my two pillars, my outcroppings, whom I am prompt to aid and love dearly."

She paused, then continued, "We will survive out enemies, visible or invisible, for I am baptized first by water, then by fire."

"And what of your dragon?" asked Hauresh, unshaken by her boldness and pointing to the lifeless heap. "It seems his life is not so precious or eternal."

"He is still alive," she reflected, "and in time, he will return to his former glory. You will see. He will make up for his sins, and he will be united again, just as we all will, we who wait patiently with fervent expectation, we who first learn to crawl, then to gnaw and bite."

Nobody in the group understood what she was talking about.

She continued, *"It is for God and for Omnipotency to do mighty things in a moment, but by degrees to grow to greatness is the course that He hath left for mankind."*

Amdusias spoke up, "And what are you? God? Omnipotency? This is blasphemy."

"Not quite, dear, but closer than you are," she answered bluntly. "I went through the cycle, and I mastered it first, you might say, but I admit my pride led to my unfortunate fall to this place...."

"But I thought you chose this place?" Hauresh asked curiously.

"I did, I do.... We all choose our place. Let us eat."

"Did somebody say eat?" said Deanis, emerging clueless from the airship wreckage. "What happened?"

Some were hesitant, and some were totally opposed to the idea, but Ashtaroth had a way about her, and she prepared the dragon over a fire to eat anyway. And soon, they were all agreeable and gnawing flesh from the dragon's bones in a feast.

"This is a high honor for him, and honor for yourselves as well," she explained after offering vows and a prayer on the feast.

And in a rare moment of humble honesty, Ashtaroth confessed that her light was not fully lit, and she said had only one regret.

Others waited for more explanation, but she went silent and looked at Hauresh. And when she saw that he was listening intently to her every word, she frowned.

"But this was my choice, to enter *through* the experience and make up for my many sins. And now I am unworthy to leave this place, and I deserve to stay longer."

Thunder cracked and lightning flashed above as she spoke.

And the rain began to fall, and Andras furrowed his brow at the absurdity of the situation, then shrugged and took another bite of the juicy dragon flesh.

After the meal, while the men were trying to repair the aircraft, Hauresh found a moment to approach Ashtaroth privately.

"You have no companion, and you speak of eternal solitude," said Hauresh. "Why not come with us?"

"I have a companion, but we will never encounter each other."

"How is that possible?" he started.

"Come, let me show you," she interrupted.

They walked down a path to a stone well, in excellent repair, with a wooden canopy overhead. A sturdy basket hung above the aperture, suspended by a pulley system with a thick white rope that wound around an axle on the side.

Hauresh wanted to speak but held his tongue while Ashtaroth released the rope lock and cranked the handle on the wheel, which turned the axle and lowered the basket deep into the well.

And after slowly drawing the bucket to the top, she whispered, *"Gamori!"* ... and on the shimmering surface of the water below appeared the image of a beautiful duchess, smiling.

"What can I do for you, Ashtaroth? And who is your visitor?" the water-spirit asked with a distant voice.

"Gamori[2], will you tell us about our future?" asked Ashtaroth.

"Oh," she asked with a smile. "True love at first sight, is it?"

"Nonsense," Hauresh and Ashtaroth both responded in sync, looked at each other and blushed.

"Oh, you," Gamori continued lightly, "still punishing yourself, are you, Ashtaroth?"

She paused and waited, but Ashtaroth was just looking down, and Hauresh looked confused and shrugged his shoulders.

Then she offered some advice. "Ashtarosh, you will remember that God's wellspring of eternal living water is found in any land. It can seem slow and painful at first, amidst surrounding peril, but with small and measured steps and *plans*," she emphasized, "and dexterity to walk the path, great fortune will result."

She continued, "When the sinner, like the wild stallion, has been tamed and trained sufficiently, then he appreciates the discipline and comes to know the mystery of God, *while still in the flesh.* And those who come to know the mystery have learned to confer benefits on others, to serve and do good for as many as possible. Nothing else is finer in the grand eternal scheme, than to be able and willing to confer these benefits and approach the Deity."

She paused for a long moment, deep in thought, then continued, *"Opposites attract and enlighten the ignorance of each other,"* she continued, "and through the discussion comes conviction... and even agreement."

"I will always be there for you," finished Gamori in a whisper. Then she smiled and vanished.

Ashtaroth sighed and locked the rope again, looking depressed. "I had hoped that she would be more specific."

Hauresh was mystified, but he gathered his wits and finally said, "Well, let us drink."

So, they took a moment to drink from the bucket with its ladle, pondering the mysteries of the Earth and her water.

Hauresh learned that the island would crumble into the sea if Ashtaroth left, and she wasn't ready to leave.

So, he made the difficult decision to leave her behind, for now. But he felt a special love for her, which was obvious to all, and she felt the same, so he swore that he would return after fulfilling his promise, assisting the others to reach their destination.

"After I return, we will decide whether to stay on the island or migrate together."

But Ashtaroth feared that he may never return.

"Can he be trusted?" she wondered to herself, but she realized there was only one way to find out.

Ashtaroth felt different now, for the light and glory of the divine presence had been lit aflame and was resting deeply within her. She now knew that she had great value to offer, and she felt a renewed childlike desire to serve others.

She went back to doing what she does best, which is to break up the foundation of the complex nature of the material world, and to focus on the purity and richness of the elements.

She smiled and laughed, resenting nothing, judging nobody, and putting things back into perspective with courage in her heart. She felt free to express herself, reflected on what she observed, and magnified both good and bad, to accelerate the inevitable.

Amdusias said a final dedicatory prayer before they prepared to leave again.

"Adonai, we turn to you in reverence to consider thy Kingdom, and to reflect how we might contribute to the Kingdom in small repetitive and cumulative ways – through the toil of labors or the intellectual pursuits, with uplifting dialog, good humor, honesty, and humility. May we serve each other and fulfill Thy divine will. We are merely dust of the earth with your breath in our souls, but we find great strength and security in THEE, our teacher and great merciful master. Thank you."

[1] אשטארות (*Ashtaroth*) is the mighty Duchess once sealed in copper by Solomon. Her eternal name is רייאל (*Reyeyael*) who is sometimes called *Zimi*. Ashtaroth is a mighty Angel who often rides on her infernal dragon, holding a Viper in her right hand, issuing forth noisome breathings and words, sometimes sweet, sometimes foul or astringent to the unprepared. She is extremely knowledgeable about many secrets and sciences, and she rules over forty legions of spirits.

Reyeyael is a masculine spirit whose fallen nature is feminine. He fell as all the great spirits fall, due to pride and ignominious failure to foresee coming events. In the long eternal run, he is self-sufficient and has no need for seeds from external sources because his legions are his seeds, and they issue forth from his five springs and return to his own bosom to regenerate eternally. And yet he falls and spends a great deal of time in a fallen state, because this is the life he wants for himself, supported by two pillars which serve as the basis or ground for his outcroppings, whom she is prompt to aid.

He declares, *"They who exercise faith will always survive their enemies, both the visible and invisible, even as I am baptized first by water, then by fire in the spirit."*

The message of Ashtaroth is conveyed through the AIR as she eternally reflects and duplicates herself.

We can taste her message in the air, and this is the message we need to consider most of all while we are in this sphere, because we have a similar fallen state and a great need for redemption, salvation, atonement, and reconciliation.

Reyeyael is prompt to aid those who will wait on him patiently (yet with fervent expectation). He is zealous, sincere in virtue, and he propagates the truth, but his pride is a stumbling block.

The truth and good motivations well up inside him to the point where he begins to ignore certain failures, so the net effect and appearance is one of fanaticism and hypocrisy, the inability or unwillingness to see his faults and shortcomings.

He wants to do too much at once, expecting everything to fall into place without incremental efforts, swallowing a meal whole.

So, he falls and is given a body to tend and nurture.

Starting as a babe, as it were, with feet in her stockings, able to balance herself with her toes, yet uncoordinated. She commits no error in the process but doesn't really move anywhere either, since she is unable to walk.

She wants to converse with those around her, especially one, whom she loves the most of all, but she struggles to initiate a meaningful interaction except through her cries and noises.

She has success in conveying some feelings but still wants more. And with some reticence, she realizes she must work patiently through one step at a time, learning to move and speak and read. There is no shortcut to the truth or the talents and relationship she wants, so she works at it incrementally.

"It is for God and for Omnipotency to see and do mighty things in a moment, but by degrees to grow to greatness is the course that he hath left for man." –Unknown

The next period of her life is a series of experiments in gnawing – biting, chewing, grinding with her teeth, masticating flesh, and consuming for nourishment. Sometimes this is disagreeable, causing discomfort in her throat and intestines, but despite the discomfort, she feels good about the union and survives.

But eventually she confronts the ambitious task of gnawing dried flesh from a bone, which is unsatisfying and difficult at first. Her legions support her efforts, pledging all their energy and resources to support the task, crafting weapons in their currency, and spraying a spirit of victory in a battle cry for good fortune.

But her light is not fully lit yet, or not fully displayed. She feels a burn from within, and a brilliant light flashes like a golden scepter swung by the gods on her behalf, as if they could predict the need for a very valiant roar and a fight in the upcoming day.

"But all will be well," the thunderous, brilliant voice calls down from above as she continues to gnaw the flesh and finds gold, yellow in color. She possesses every quality she needs at this point in time to accomplish the task in her current position, because she recognizes the severe potential for danger and peril. So, she exercises correctness.

And despite her correctness, she must still undergo a painful experience as a result of her fall and her desire to enter through the experience, to make up for her sins. And yet she makes the pain even worse because she punishes herself unnecessarily, feeling unworthy, depriving her senses and emotions.

These constraints she places upon herself are a rite of passage, which fully enforce and implement the law.

The object in her mouth was a blockade and prevented normal breathing and unification of the jaws and mouth, so she gnawed through to remove the obstacle. In so doing, the high heavens and low earth likewise come together to a sound understanding, with force and a *legal basis* to ensure conformity and future compliance; agreed-upon rules of engagement.

The thunder usually follows the lightning but in this case the order is reversed, as the thunder rolls first and paves the way for the light to flash without any reverberation, so the result is bright intelligence, which follows great movement.

As a result of this sequence of events, there is balance for a time, as the ruler in heaven practices judgment tempered by leniency. Penalties are invoked with prudence and patience; intelligence and laws are promulgated by the public servants who readily see the intelligence of these laws. These proceedings are majestic, and a pattern of order is established for review and comment, due to the bright light immediately cast upon the event.

[2] Ashtaroth's spiritual companion is גמורי (*Gamori*), the duke who also appears in the form of a duchess, a beautiful form with a crown upon his head (or "about his waist" according to some), sometimes riding atop his great camel.

He knows about all things past, present, and future, and he freely speaks about them, knowing the faith of future generations and hearing their cries like the dust of the earth were rising in chorus. So, he speaks of hidden treasures, and he assists boys and men to obtain love.

His true name is פויאל (*Povyael*), and he supports the universe with pride yet also an agreeable modesty and humor which everybody enjoys. He is not worried about fame because this comes easily to him, along with good fortune and philosophy. He fulfills requests and serves as a great prophet and seer, bringing the word of truth in simple symbols and telepathically, trusting God to raise up a suitable mouthpiece on his behalf to support him in his efforts.

Somewhat ironically, his calling is to spread the word and convince others of the word of salvation, hope, and faith in the Redeemer and Savior, but he does so with a certain respect for silence and reverence, allowing others to do most of the talking.

Working in tandem with his master, he converts the weaknesses of the faithful – those with contrite hearts and repentant spirits – into strengths, in fulfillment of ancient covenants.

His fall was terrible like all the rest, but he had the peace of mind to realize his forsaken condition and beseech the Lord for help. He was dug deeply into the ground like a well of muddy water, undrinkable even by the birds and other beasts.

So, he began to break down and cry, feeling unredeemable and dejected by all, and his walls began to crumble. There was no help from above, and he felt like a broken, discarded basket, unable to hold any water. The water escaped and flowed away, nourishing only the shrimp in grasshoppers nearby in the grass.

Eventually he achieved homeostasis with the soil of the earth, and with surrounding creatures that fill the gaps in his structure, so he felt some integrity. And he gained a sense of continence, feeling healthy and whole, due to a series complex yet simple symbiotic relationships with lifeforms and seals between them.

He gained clarity within his mind, but unfortunately the full potential was still mostly untapped and unused. So, he still felt sorrowful about his situation, and he wished the king would put him to better use.

So, he cultivated himself, not concerned nor aware of others for a while. His lining was well laid, and he felt healthy and capable – in good repair – and so, he carried on in virtual solitude with no criticisms nor condemnation, but with no real praise either.

He finally began to experience great joy in his life after others found the well and drew from his waters freely.

His water supply is cold and clear and limpid. People recognize and honor him as a good governor and a leader due to his clarity and willingness to share.

His water is freely available, seemingly inexhaustible in supply.

The entire country is cleansed by his light, intelligent influence, like a body imbibing pure water.

Epilogue

The First Book

of

The

144,000

"The Watchful One and the Tree of Life"

The entire Qabalistic tree is also an image of mankind and the individual man, the symbol of oneself, which allows us to enter into the mysteries objectively, since it is impossible to analyze ourselves directly. We do so through the tree and its analogies, which are limitless and profound.

The major symbol is the tree itself, the Tree of Life.

To walk toward the tree and partake of its fruit is to enter into a relationship with Deity, becoming one with his covenant people.

It is a straight and narrow path, so our responsibility is to hold carefully to the iron rod (the Word of God) leading to the Tree.

Being obedient to God's word implies that we can hear the word in the first place, and that we can see his guiding light. And this has never been more important in all the history of mankind, because this is the final dispensation, a time when children are severed from the Spirit at a young age, too young to remember, due to the competing and complex voices which bombard our minds for control.

Many of us are desperate for identity and control, so we are prone to making disjointed decisions as we wrestle for some meaning and relevance in this massively confusing life.

The Tree of Life is a stable metaphor to help us get a grip and start walking along the covenant path.

The covenant path is symbolized by obedience to ordinances, such as baptism by immersion in water, but this is just an initial step to start the process of obedience, which begins with faith in the One whose works are mighty to save.

The central sphere of the Qabalah is the Christ, who is the most connected and beautiful (תפארת), known as Vehuviah in the book.

The Qabalah is intended to be, from its inception, a medium or channel for the living Word in its most intense and sincere form.

It is the word which humbles us to repent and return to the Lord, and to set aside our pride and treat others as equal companions who have the same set of commandments and tasks as we have: to humble ourselves, build Zion, love ourselves and others, etc.

The plan of the Architect obviously will not be frustrated in any meaningful way, so our best approach is to move forward with faith in that plan and its founder, also our savior and redeemer, who knows true value and worth and potential for good as we embrace his word and his will.

The ten Sephiroth are collectively the heavenly man (עילאה אדם) or primordial being (אדם קדמון), whose mind also created and nurtured all the holy living creatures.

Their connecting link is the breath (רוח) of life, which is the hidden influence upon which the four principal holy creatures (taurus, leo, scorpio, aquarius; i.e., bull, lion, eagle, and man) all depend and communicate.

And so, we find a miraculous balance (מתקלא) which provides good soil for the holy tree of life (עץ החיים) and a foundation for the worlds (עולם), which wrap around and feed into the source.

These worlds are described in terms of intelligence, morality, and finally, materiality.

The balance of the tree is in part due to its endowment of free will to its agents, but the master of the orchard also takes an active role in nurturing the tree, splicing, digging, transplanting, harvesting, pruning the bad and unwieldy, etc., to preserve the root of the tree, and to save as many good branches as possible.

We are mere servants in the orchard, commanded by the master, yet we can play an active role in the process, communicating our observations and requests actively and assertively.

The master listens, but more importantly he commands, and we must listen and execute as commanded. The concept of tuning into higher intelligence and receiving revelation from the higher worlds is the subject of the remainder of this series.

How can one hear and recognize the spirit? Why should we?

We start with the low hanging fruit.

Part of the dilemma we face as human beings is that despite our royal heritage, we are caught in the fallen state, this world or plane of action (עשיה), which is possessed in no small degree by demons and shells (קליפות) whose husbandman is Satan or Samael (סמאל), who is also the angel of poison and death.

He systematically brings pain, destruction, and disease to the planet to ensure his own survival, allowed by the master to exist for a period of time. Consider the vineyard in which the master knowingly allows some tares, weeds, and fruitless branches to thrive in their hosts, because to remove them suddenly would shock and kill the good parts, which ironically have a symbiotic relationship with their evil cousins.

The wife of Samael is known as Eisheth Zenunim (אשת זנונים), and together they comprise the Beast (חיוא).

And the result of this beast ruling the roost is a predicament in which the reign of terror, shock, and fear is the norm.

The world is diseased by complacency, dishonesty, disharmony, and lack of integrity; perfect conditions for the beast to thrive. Speculators and charlatans thrive as well, since they gang up with other idiots who feel comforted and entertained by the chaos and mayhem.

So, this terrible environment is obviously distracting from the original source of all the action, which is eternal beauty and beautiful creation.

The archetypal and creative worlds are veiled from our minds, except through spiritual quickening, and the formative world is also outside (or inside) our normal view.

We live and breathe in what appears to be a world of action, cause and effect, laws of physics, etc., but this is an illusion. Right beyond the veil is the angelic formative world, a world without heavy matter, whose beings wear luminous garments over their intelligent identities. This is a good place to center our thoughts and begin to climb the tree, to seek the higher fruit.

Humility is a key part of this process, a meek approach to accept the word of service and love, hope, faith, charity, kindness, etc.

The process of becoming humble is one of accessing the root of the soul – spiritual over carnal – and following commandments.

Healing is available to all who will merely look, and observe the snake or virus raised up on the staff. This requires laying aside vain and false hopes, which is a distraction from clear vision.

We can enhance our clarity by engaging the other senses as well. For example, we can write, draw, take notes, or otherwise express ourselves, and take control of our bodies and minds.

This is not necessarily complex or difficult, it just requires following through on a train of thought fluidly, with faith and a willingness to listen, then conveying the message as it is heard.

At this point we have traveled ten steps and experienced a "type" of the final destination, but we are left in a frenzy and will be controlled by the adversary unless we take the steps.

So, take the steps!

8338c938-bee0-4825-849a-9f9dfc6bd986R01